THE FROST
ON HIS SHOULDERS

Lorenzo Mediano

THE FROST
ON HIS SHOULDERS

*Translated from the Spanish
by Lisa Dillman*

Europa
editions

Europa Editions
214 West 29th Street
New York, N.Y. 10001
www.europaeditions.com
info@europaeditions.com

Translation by Lisa Dillman
Original title: *La escarcha sobre los hombros*
Translation copyright © 2012 by Europa Editions

Library of Congress Cataloging in Publication Data is available
ISBN 978-1-60945-072-4

Mediano, Lorenzo
The Frost on His Shoulders

Book design and cover illustration by Emanuele Ragnisco
www.mekkanografici.com

Prepress by Grafica Punto Print – Rome

Printed in the USA

CONTENTS

THE FROST
ON HIS SHOULDERS

Several weeks ago, an unknown editor at the *Aragon Herald* devoted half a column to the events that occurred in our region. No doubt, this half a column went unnoticed by almost all of the paper's readership, not just because it was buried deep on an inside page, lost among other stories from towns as tiny and insignificant as ours, but also because educated citizens consider a speech by Lerroux, by Azaña, by Largo Caballero or any one of the other politicians who govern—or perhaps I should say divide—this long-suffering Republic to be more important than any amount of blood that might be spilled in the villages woven throughout our landscape. Unless, of course, the peasants' blood can be used as a weapon against political adversaries, as it was two years ago, in suppressing the Casas Viejas uprising, in Andalucía.

We ourselves almost didn't find out about it either, not for lack of interest, but simply because I'm the only one in town who reads the paper, every other day. I'm sure readers will find it odd that a rural teacher's salary, which barely pays enough to eat, allows me to buy the paper, even if it is only every two days. Let me explain: when Don Casildo Baldellou was young, he set off to study in Zaragoza and spent considerable time there; but then his brother, the heir, died, and he had to return to take charge of the family home. His time in the city and his truncated education bestowed upon him a certain intellectual prestige and standing above the other townspeople, a prestige that he bolsters by having the paper delivered to him by horseback. He does it out of sheer bumptiousness, given that running his household long ago wrested away the sophisticated diversion of reading; but every Saturday he still brings the newspaper to the bar where folks gather and, donning his glasses, reads aloud any random news story from the front page so that afterward, at the regulars' respectful silence, he can declare, "I don't know where it's all going to end!"

Be that as it may, his presumptuous little display—like his glasses, I might add: he's got near-perfect vision and doesn't need them now nor will he ever—suits Don Felipe the priest and yours truly just fine. Once Don Casildo has reaffirmed his erudite pre-eminence over the masses, the papers become useless to him, so he donates them to the priest and me, and the two of us split them equitably. In a sense, this is a bribe, since it's understood that if we want the steady stream of papers to continue, we must never undermine Don Casildo's ruse, and that when he declares "I don't know where it's all going to end!" we respectfully nod, as if his pronouncement simultaneously captured the wisdom of both the Church Fathers and philosopher Giner de los Ríos.

For this low price, I get to read half the news from Spain and abroad and, with a bit of imagination, I fill in the other half as if I were doing a crossword. I don't really mind the two or three-week delay. It just feels like I inhabit another world, a world that's a bit slower, a bit calmer; and when I get disturbing news, I know that it's already days old and, for better or for worse, it now pertains to the past.

At any rate, as luck would have it, the half column of text that initially gave rise to what I'm now writing, corresponded to the priest's section. Personally, I've been harboring suspicions for some time that Don Felipe doesn't actually read his portion of the paper but uses it as fireplace kindling. For him not to notice such an important story only corroborates my theory.

At any rate, an émigré from our town who now resides in Huesca—Miguelón, third son of Joaquín Naval—read the piece, clipped it, and mailed it to his father. Joaquín Naval reads enough to realize that the half-column was about our town, though he couldn't ascertain exactly what it said, which is why he brought it to the *tertulia* that night at the bar.

Don Casildo's reputation as local intellectual elite teetered and nearly nose-dived when he was presented with this story he knew nothing about, and he could do nothing but repeat, "I don't know where it's all going to end!" like some kind of incantation.

At this point I stepped in, fearful that if Don Casildo's stature as local sage foundered, he might stop buying the paper. So I explained to everyone that the Huesca edition of the Aragón *Herald* is not the same as the Zaragoza edition, just as Cariñena wine doesn't taste the same as Somontano wine, although we use the same word for them both. The *Herald* that Don Casildo gets is the Zaragoza edition, which is higher quality, as befits a man of his schooling, while the clipping in question came from the Huesca edition, which as we all know is a city of lesser importance.

And since Zaragoza is an important metropolis, it doesn't concern itself with matters that take place in remote townships such as our own.

Needless to say, this is all a lie, but even though the cleverest folks sensed that my reasoning was none too solid, no one dared contradict me on issues of culture. So Don Casildo, donning his useless spectacles, read the piece slowly, as a religious silence descended on those congregated.

Oh, the travails of a journalist! One night he's faced with a blank space and the editor-in-chief tells him to write something, anything, doesn't matter what, as long as it will interest idle readers; the journalist pores over court reports and finds a case in which love, hate, and blood intermingle; he reads the version the judge has accepted as accurate, which in turn was based on the Guardia Civil report, which was a collection of local residents' depositions—in many cases biased and contradictory and to a large extent suppressed because they pertained to dark family secrets and questions of revenge that were nobody's business. From all of this he must bang out a story that, although it will never be true, must at least seem so.

Then the editor-in-chief will change a few sentences to make the piece more interesting and the layout editor will strike a paragraph or two to make the short, last-minute story fit. And only then will the reader, having purchased the paper—or in my case having sat through Don Casildo's theatrical performance—be able to read the hazy vestige of what truly happened. And he'll consider himself well informed, au courant with what's going on in the world.

So it's no surprise that the journalist's story bore only a vague resemblance to what actually happened here in town.

Scarcely had Don Casildo removed his spectacles and

pronounced his fêted "I don't know where it's all going to end!" when a torrent of indignation was unleashed. Those who'd been named in the article flew off the handle and cursed, undaunted by the presence of Father Felipe, which usually tempered such outbursts; by contrast, those who'd taken part in the events without having their names appear felt scorned. This caricature of our town was an offense to each and every inhabitant.

Anger overflowed the confines of the tiny bar where we were gathered and soon, as though drawn by a mysterious force, the previously absent residents all assembled. Women forgot about making dinner and came to scream and insult; old people did, too, though they could do nothing but shake their canes and look for a place to rest their crooked spines; and children, though perplexed as to what was going on, found the excitement in the air contagious and added to the confusion by yelling and jumping up and down. Even the men from Casa Carrasquero showed up, and that's half an hour away, and the ones from Casa Simó, who have to cross Grallaro Creek to get here.

There was urgency in the air, a need to do something, to find a release for their indignation, but alas! There was no Bastille to storm, no guilty party to sacrifice in collective catharsis, no action that the hardened, weather-beaten calloused hands could undertake. Some paced up and down the street as if in search of an enemy; others demanded to see the fateful clipping and eyeballed it again and again, as if that would somehow enable them to decipher the otherwise incomprehensible letters; most simply clenched their impotent fists.

Finally our mayor, Sebastián Badías, of Casa Bardal, proposed that we restore the town's honor by committing to paper what had actually happened, so the city folks would know the truth. The proposal was welcomed with a cry of jubilation. The town council met quickly to decide upon practical details while the rest of the townsfolk respectfully exited the packed bar to allow deliberations to take place with the necessary calm; and they waited outside in a silence even more awesome and menacing than their earlier uproar had been. Since this was a matter of culture, I was invited to the plenary session, as was Don Casildo, whose reputation was now at no risk whatsoever, since no one doubted that his Zaragoza paper was vastly superior to the Huesca paper, which published such fabricated stories.

In theory, the task of composing a reply to the insult was assigned to Don Casildo, a townsman by birth and not by adoption, as am I; but he excused himself by remarking that, although he was perfectly capable of writing it, the numerous obligations he had to his inherited estate would impede him from dedicating sufficient time to the task. Everyone concurred that the care of livestock and land was more important than the negligibly productive task of teaching children to read and write. After all, people can go their whole lives without learning their letters; not so without eating.

And thus it was decided that, until the reply to the newspaper was finished, school would be closed in the afternoon with the aim of providing me the necessary time to compose it. Likewise, the township would provide me with as much free paper and ink as I might require for the task.

I tried to explain that whatever had taken place in our town mattered to no one but us during this turbulent month of November 1934, with the events of Asturias and Cataluña still so recent; that our town's name would have been forgotten even by the no-good journalist who wrote the absurd piece—if he'd ever remembered it to begin with—, that some sorrows it's best not to stir up and instead let them lie in pious oblivion. But given how worked up everyone was, they paid no heed to my warnings, and I considered it prudent not to be too insistent.

Leaving school at lunchtime the following day, I was approached by Pilar, of Casa Bardal, (which, by the way, is one of the town's most powerful households), who relayed her father's invitation to lunch and told me not to forget to bring paper and writing implements.

Since everyone knows that a teacher's salary doesn't pay enough to live on, it's not unusual for the most important houses to invite me to their table from time to time, while the poorer ones are happy to send a few eggs or vegetables my way now and then.

To my surprise, however, instead of the typical stew of beans, vegetables, potatoes and bacon eaten most days in every house, I was presented with a delicious dish of *codas*. For those who don't know what *codas* are, let me say that when female lambs are born in summertime, their tails are docked in early November so the males can more easily inseminate them; these tails, cooked in an almond sauce, are a delicacy only the richest can afford. That the dish is so rare makes it tremendously desirable. I had never tasted it before, and being served such a meal indicated a desire to shower me with a luxury far above my modest social standing.

After the exquisite meal, the mayor asked me to take up pen and paper and transcribe his version of the events pertaining to his household that were mentioned in the article.

In vain I attempted to explain that if we wanted the

paper to publish any sort of correction, we needed to be concise, to leave out sort of minor details so important to us but excessive and bothersome to the average reader, who doesn't care how we dress, how much land we own, or whether we're worried about a mule that's gone lame. Of course, yes, all of this is important for them to be able to truly understand us and, consequently, determine why what happened, happened; nevertheless, deep down, the people who buy the newspaper don't really want to understand at all; they want the illusion of knowledge, without actually taking the time needed to acquire it.

My postulating was all in vain. Obediently, fully aware of the fact that no paper would publish such a verbose outpouring, I took down what I was told on the paper donated by the township, in fair payment for the exquisite meal. And to my shame, I allowed my pen to transcribe not only the superfluous—which would have been forgivable—but also the lies that attempted to conceal the hatred in people's hearts.

In the days that followed, invitation after invitation, I visited every house in town. I don't know if it was by prior arrangement or some strange social instinct was at work, but they followed strict hierarchical order. First, the most powerful casas: after Casa Bardal I was called to Casa Torrera, Casa Simó, Casa Sopera, Casa Nariñós . . . ; then came the more modest casas, beginning with Casa Badiello and after which came Casa La Selva, Casa Mozcós, Casa Alins, Casa Mateu . . .

It took over a month to visit each and every house in the town and surrounding areas, and in each one I ate lavish meals, drank the best wine and listened to the inhabitants' long-winded tales. It was like a monotonous, repetitive symphony, full of good intentions and naiveté. And it was all false, even more false than the journalist's initial half-column.

The day after finishing at the last house, the invitations ceased and I discovered a warm plate of food at the schoolhouse door. I realized that the townspeople now expected me to compose what they'd told me. So, I locked myself in my room and pretended to write. Yes, that's right, I say I pretended to write, because after thirty-eight visits, I had in my hands over two hundred utterly confusing, contradictory pages, impossible for anyone to decipher—even if they actually had the patience required to read them and understood the Aragonese dialect in which they were written. What's more, I couldn't omit anything without offending whoever had recounted it to me, and in a small town, an insult of that sort is not easily forgiven. Given that my survival depends on the good will of my neighbors, the reader will understand why it was necessary for me to exercise extreme caution.

I was perfectly aware of the fate that would await those pages once they reached the editor's desk, even if I did—at great risk to my sustenance—attempt to abridge them into a hundred, or fifty, or ten pages. So instead I opted to pretend I was writing, when in fact I spent the afternoons reading one of my very few books; and when I deemed that sufficient time had passed, I presented the mayor with the selfsame notes I'd taken when I first did the rounds from house to house.

The whole town was convened, then, and Don Casildo—glasses donned, standing on the town hall balcony—began reading that impenetrable gibberish, incomprehensible to anyone who wasn't part of our community, while the townspeople gathered in the plaza listened in a respectful silence with an almost religious attitude.

For hours and hours, Don Casildo read out what each person had dictated to me; and, just as I'd predicted, everyone found it satisfactory. They understood nothing about the structure required for literary composition; nor did they realize that no stranger could know if "Don Mariano's Alba" was in fact the man's wife, mother, or daughter; nor did anyone grasp the fact that although for them the strength, health, castration, shoeing, age and teeth of their livestock are vital to a tale, a city-dweller is entirely indifferent as to whether a mule is dappled or dun or badly shoed. No, they were just hearing a description of the town and its inhabitants as they saw them, that is, an enormously congratulatory description of themselves. And set against this gilded backdrop, one man personified all manner of evil, all vice, all perversion; one man comprised the miniscule black stain that makes the whiteness of the sheet stand out all the more; one man was the sole guilty party in the events that earned our town its sad notoriety and a half-column on an inside page of the Aragón Herald, Huesca edition.

As though in a trance, they thus exorcized the demons that had been tormenting them for the past few months; for a lie, if shared by every member of the community, becomes first credible, then possible, and finally true. Thus in perverse communion, they stood calmly and quietly for hours, hardly even gesturing except to nod every now and again at the most important—and most fallacious—passages, until Don Casildo finally finished and took off his glasses. No one, except me, realized that for once he hadn't made his famous declaration, but there was a collective sigh, as if a weight had been removed, unburdening their hearts. I could almost hear an "amen" more sincere than all those uttered at Sunday mass: so be it, so be it, so be it.

After the ceremony, the pages were carefully packed up and sent off with the weekly mail. And from that moment on, every day that went by, people said, "It must have gotten to Barbastro by now," or, "It's probably in Huesca," or, "They must be reading it at the paper by now."

And starting on the day that people thought they must be reading it at the paper by now, everyone was overcome with uneasiness, because nobody could imagine what it is that people do at a newspaper, or how long it takes to print the news. They couldn't say, "It must be at the typesetter's by now" or, "They're probably doing the layout by now" because no one knew what a typesetter was or what it meant to lay out a page; I, too, feigned ignorance to avoid inconvenient questions. Thus commenced a nerve-wracking wait.

For the first time in his life, Don Casildo read from start to finish the weekly papers he had delivered every week, which required devoting Fridays and Saturdays to the task. The neighbors, in turn, seeing the generous sacrifice he was making for the community, scythed his fields for free, and herded his livestock, in an attempt to compensate him in some way.

When Don Casildo finished reading on Saturday nights, he'd head to the bar where the entire village anxiously awaited him, and sadly shake his head. Then everyone would return home, downcast, without Don Casildo even having mustered the spirit to read out a story to them, now of all times, when he just about knew the news by heart and there were so many he could have remarked upon.

Finally, in February, everyone lost all hope of their version of events being published. And since they couldn't imagine that the journalists were simply uninterested, their guilty consciences took it to mean that somehow, mysteriously, the lies professed in the manuscript had been found out. And then, since someone had dared to question their accepted truth, that truth lost its sway and its ability to ward off their blood-spattered ghosts.

One Saturday, Don Casildo went back to passing comment on a news story each week and proclaiming, "I don't know where it's all going to end!" and the people went back to the fields, called to work by the coming of spring, and the old folks went back to sitting in the sun and declaring that times weren't what they used to be. But deep in their hearts, they couldn't fool themselves.

Even I felt uneasy because I, more than anyone, know—or think I know—what really happened. Me, who more than anyone should have challenged the lies—and yet I prostituted my pen out of fear.

I was still in possession of the paper that the township had given me to write the final draft of the events they'd recounted, and one night, in the middle of the night, amid horrible nightmares, I got out of bed, drenched in sweat, and, lighting an oil lamp, began to write the truth. The truth that I bore witness to, and that no one wants to hear.

Now that the days are getting longer, I make the most of the sunlight—these are no times for squandering lamp oil in vain—and, rather than go for my evening walk, I write a few pages.

If anyone ever reads this humble chronicle of the deeds

both terrible and beautiful that befell a small town at the foot of the Pyrenees, let it be known that they were penned by a schoolteacher who wants only to be at peace with himself. And that peace can come only from the truth, even if the people don't want to see it.

CHAPTER II

T he place where the events I'm going to recount took place is called Biescas de Obago. Don't confuse it, dear reader—as the postman sometimes does when delivering what little mail comes our way— with the famous Biescas (sans add-ons) in the Valley of Tena, although ours, too, is a Pyrenean cattle town. Much smaller still, and surely unknown to the reader—unless he's a hunting enthusiast—is another Biescas, nestled in the Valley of Bardají. This isn't the one I'm referring to either. And finally, near us, lies Biescas de Obarra, in the Valley of Isábena, near the once-important Convent of Obarra, now abandoned and in ruins. The geographical proximity of Biescas de Obarra and the appreciable similarity between that town's name and our own leads to even those living relatively close-by confusing the two.

The Biescas in question, our town, is located on a sunny hill some four hundred yards from the river. Yes, I know the name and the fact that sun shines on the town constitute a contradiction, given that "obago" means "shady place" in Aragonese, but there you have it. And though I'm neither a historian nor a linguist, I've got my own theory about the nomenclature: less than thirty minutes down the road is one of the many east-west ridges running through the Pyrenees foothills—the Suerri ridge. Its peak—though it's not very high nor do geographers consider it important enough to include on large-scale maps—projects cool shade all across its northern slope, and that shade, although hindering crop growth and favoring the an accumulation of snow in the winter, also keeps the grass green during even the most prolonged droughts. And that fact, I'm convinced, is important enough to a town so dependent on grazing as to merit appending it to the name.

Since the protagonist of much of this tale is a shepherd, I should also add that our town's flocks are particularly fortunate, in that they're not transhumant. For towns higher up, closer to the mountain passes, transhumance—seasonal migration, that is—is a necessary evil, since the snow blankets their grazing ground in the winter. Here, on the other hand, most flocks are "standing", that is, they stay in one place all year. In the summertime, there's enough communal grassland on the mountain for everyone; and in wintertime the valley meadows (and cut hay on snowy days) can feed a lot of cattle. Of all the wealthy houses, the only ones to go down to the valley are the Casa Mariñós flock—and that's just because they have vast property holdings in Tamarite—and the Casa Sopena flock, because they've had usufruct rights on the Zuera municipal district's grazing land since time immemorial. Generally, not having enough land to graze them, smaller herds belonging to poorer households have to band together and migrate in the winter. But I'll refrain from launching into greater detail about the municipal district, so as not to risk being seized by the same rural spirit I criticized in the last chapter and getting lost in some elaborate, long-winded portrayal of the region; otherwise I'd end up talking about the cool, shady streams that never dry up, and are dedicated to San Antonio because they say horses' sores heal faster when washed in their water. Or I might speak of our fertile cereal-growing land, where wheat is planted every other year and comes out better the closer it is to the river, even if an occasional flood comes and ruins it. Or the vegetable gardens close to town where we sometimes get late tomatoes, though they have to be tended carefully and don't always thrive. Or how on the sunniest slopes, which have been terraced for generations, we get a few olive trees, almond trees, and grape vines that sometimes bear fruit that, on its own, the climate would never permit.

Allow me to disregard such details, which a farmer or rancher would no doubt find both indispensable and fascinating, but for city readers must be tiresome and even irksome.

I'll submit to their tastes and dispositions, since I imagine that city folks are the only ones who might take the time to read these lines (if, that is, they're ever read by anyone). Country folks occupy their spare time in other ways: when night falls they mull over their loves and hates while gazing into the fire rather than engaging in the forbidden—to them—art of reading.

For the citified to understand my text, I'll have to translate the words spoken by the protagonists into sentences they themselves wouldn't understand if they read them—or, I should say, if they heard them, given that the majority are almost illiterate. But it's a necessary artifice, and in deference to my readers, I'll put words they never said—but would have said, since they felt them in their hearts—into their mouths. Hill talk is a mixture of facial expressions and silences, looks that mean a million things or none, miniscule gestures that can be threatening or friendly, sighs that—depending on how deep they are—might signify one thing or another. And since they've known each other since childhood, that's what folks use to speak of love and hate, friendship and power; they forge alliances and inflict mortal wounds; ride people hard or neglect them like fallow fields. What literary genius could possibly translate so subtle a language within the narrow limits of the page? Certainly not the humble schoolteacher of a miserable, rural school who is only writing to unburden his conscience and cry out—albeit belatedly—against the anguish brought on by the blood that soaked the forest's black humus, and the lies that tried to bury it.

So, dear reader, you must know that despite my limited talent, I can transmit only a vague and hazy version of what happened. But if there's one thing you can trust, it's that I shall be sincere.

To make this story of love, greed, and hate intelligible, I'll also have to explain what the word *casa* means, in this text, and in the towns of the Pyrenees. It's not a house. No, not the house that's a building made of stone for the rich or adobe for the more humble. Here, houses—*casas*—are everything: the thick walls, vaulted cellars, flagstone roofs, and closed bedrooms; but also the people who inhabit them, the land, the animals, the sharecroppers, the servants, children born there, beasts of burden, tools and implements, oil for the lamps, vines and fruit trees, and even the paltry or considerable savings stashed away through sacrifice to purchase a mule or buy medicine.

When children are born here, they receive surnames from each of their parents, because that's the law and the state requires it. But this is a gift seldom used: when drafted or married, say, or if land is bought or sold before a notary, or when there's a census or an election. Aside from these sporadic occasions, surnames are irrelevant, and no one uses them to identify people, because what really matters is what house they belong to. Even the interested party when required to use family names, seems to waver and doubt, as though unsure who that was, as though self-conscious and unnatural, dressed in church clothes.

People belong to a specific house, a *casa*, from birth, and this seems so obvious to everyone that they deem it more important than their parents' surnames. Sometimes it causes considerable confusion to outsiders, and I myself, when I first arrived, took quite some time to figure out who was who, and had to stop calling children at school by their last names.

Only one person can rule the house, and his authority is tyrannical, absolute and unquestionable. It's patriarchy in its purest form: the head of the household, referred to as "the master," is more like a feudal lord than a doting grandfather or affectionate parent, and he exerts his power not only over his own children but over the farmhands and beasts of burden, too. I don't know whether this repressive family structure is found in other parts of Spain as well or if it's exclusive to the Pyrenees. I suppose the rugged climate and landscape make this cruel reality a necessity for survival.

In order to avoid breaking up the estate, the master selects an heir from among his descendants. You might say that this is not unusual, and that it means we don't end up with the pernicious smallholders who've wreaked such havoc in other parts of Spain; and that—for instance—in

Cataluña, too, the first-born inherits everything. But what's distinctive here is that the father is free to disregard birth order in selecting his heir, and in exceptional cases might even choose a daughter or granddaughter as successor. Not only that, but he can also change his mind at will, thereby condemning the previously selected heir—who had already prepared to assume power—to poverty. And this, as you can surely see, grants the father—or grandfather—absolute command.

Those not selected to be heirs have different fates, depending on whether they belong to wealthy houses or poor ones. Those from rich houses are educated and thus able to choose liberal professions, join the military, or become priests. Those from poorer houses can either remain part of the household as *tiones* (or *tionas* if they're female)—disinherited siblings—go to work for a wealthier house, or set off for greener pastures. The women, if they are beautiful, can aspire to marry the heir of a poor house.

When I think of the *tiones* it breaks my heart, for they're like a tree's barren branches. They sit at the same table as their more fortunate brothers, but that's where all privilege ends. They work sunup to sundown for nothing but basic sustenance, clothing when absolutely necessary and, if it's been a good year, a little tobacco. And so it goes, day after day, serving first their fathers, then their brothers, then their nephews . . . until they grow old. Then they'll be given lighter chores, like making honeycomb cells from straw and dung, or caring for children, or collecting firewood kindling . . . And finally, one day, with a sigh of relief, they get to rest forever.

Unwritten rules on relations between a disinherited sibling and his house stipulate that he must never marry, under penalty of immediate expulsion. The harsh environment we live in is what requires that it be that way, for a house can support only one family.

Siblings who don't want to—or can't—stay on at their houses go to work as shepherds or servants for more powerful households. This allows them to earn a little money of their own, but not enough to start a family. So, in exchange for a salary, which affords them a few pleasures, their situation is much more precarious, so if they fall ill or have an accident they may find themselves out on a limb. Toward the end of their lives when their strength is failing, they'll donate themselves and the pittance they've saved to the house where they've always worked, and then keep working there for free—to the degree they're able—until they die.

Now, if you're wondering why the younger ones don't learn trades and become carpenters, masons or cobblers, let me explain that those skills are jealously guarded within a few poor houses with no land or cattle to speak of, so they pass their legacy on exclusively to their heirs.

Finally, those *tiones* unwilling to choose one of these two fates bundle up their clothes, throw in a loaf of bread and a few coins, and set out to seek their fortunes. Few are those who dare to leave, fewer still those who improve their station. There are stories told of audacious men who triumphed in Zaragoza, Barcelona, even America; but I know how hard it is for a semi-illiterate peasant to succeed, and I think despite their aspirations, they do, too, and that's why they're reconciled to putting up with the grueling days.

So, what happens when love wells up in one of these

poor *tiones*, despite all the backbreaking work, and it's a love stronger than the house that feeds, protects and controls him? Everyone and everything contrives to destroy it, for it's a threat to the community's very survival. It simply won't be tolerated. And not out of any prudish concept of morality, because everyone (except Don Felipe) accepts that when the physical urge is great enough, a boy might pay a few *reales* to Jacinta of Casa Alins, or Carmen of Casa Mozcós, to find relief without fear of fathering a child. No, what's really dangerous is the idea that love might subvert the social order that guarantees survival in a place where nature is so implacable.

But when men and women from these parts feel something, they're as obstinate in their feelings as they are in toiling the poor land that scarcely enables them to get by, year after year. They might suffer in silence for a very long time, hardly a sign or a gleam in their eye betraying their firm determination.

Little by little, though, love and hate will begin to intermingle until one day, none of us can any longer pretend we didn't see it, or feign that nothing was going on because no one said a word. And then, with the same country instinct that enables us to sense the coming rain, we'll all know that soon there will be blood.

Chapter III

When I composed the first, fallacious version of events, everyone swore that Ramón of Casa Badiello had proven he was a perverse and twisted individual all the way back in the tender days of his youth. To support the claim, they cited his penchant for stealing fruit from trees, or recounted pranks such as drinking the communion wine—jealously guarded by Don Felipe—when he was an altar boy; they said he let out the sow belonging to señora Antonia of Casa Mateu and rode her like a horse, which earned him a bite that almost tore off his calf. In order to stress his lewd nature, they even recalled that, along with a few other boys, he used to try to peek inside the inn where muleteers spent the night on their way up to the mountain passes. The inn, which is part of Casa Mozcós, is also where Carmen lives, Carmen being an orphan who was taken in there and now sells her body as service to the inn's lodgers, as well as to the *tiones*, shepherds and town hands who, by forgoing some other need, manage to put aside the two pesetas she charges.

To all of this I say: nonsense; it's all nonsense! What child has never stolen a piece of fruit? And not just out of hunger but for the sheer thrill of the forbidden. It's a minor infraction, and one that's traditionally been tolerated—provided the kids don't take anything back to their houses—though custom dictates that the owner fume and look surly, that he shout and perhaps even show signs of giving chase.

And as far as mischief is concerned, let's not even discuss it. Kids from rich houses—who've got the time to plot evil deeds—get up to a lot more than those from poor houses, who have to work all day. And as far as Carmen is concerned, folks would do well to keep their mouths shut and be ashamed of themselves. It's only natural for boys to be curious, especially when they hear adults whisper and carry on as if it were all a big mystery; if he spied on Carmen, it was nothing the other boys didn't do, too. It's the adults who ought to be blushing: it's us who allowed an orphan to end up like that, with no one so much as protesting simply because she didn't belong to any house and thus had no one to defend her. Not so for Jacinta of Casa Alins. It's true that Casa Alins is a poor—more than poor—house, and that the pesetas Jacinta brings in helped them buy a pair of mules, without which they'd have starved to death; but Jacinta also does what she does because she doesn't want to work like other women. Though to be honest, I ought to add that she used to have a boyfriend, quite a dashing head shepherd, who disappeared when she got pregnant. When it comes right down to it, though, Jacinta has brothers, and she can take a stroll without being stoned by gangs of kids hurling insults— insults whose meaning and nastiness is beyond their comprehension.

I had Ramón in school for just three years, and I can readily declare that I saw nothing odd about him. A bright kid with blue eyes—very handsome despite his dirty face—, he very quickly learned what little I had time to teach him. And it truly pained me when he was eight years old that his family sent him to work as a shepherd's boy. Ah, well, I guess everyone knows that childhood is short-lived when you grow up in a poor house.

"What a life those shepherds's boys lead nowadays!" old head shepherds cry, their voices tinged with envy. You see, forty or fifty years ago there were no trained dogs, none of that furry breed of clever, canine shepherds to guide the flock at the human's beck and call. Back then, their only form of help were Pyrenees mastiffs, ferocious watchdogs that kept the flock safe from wolves and thieves, their necks adorned with collars that were spiked with nails. But since there are fewer and fewer wolves these days, shepherds don't value loyal watchdogs as much.

The work now done by trained dogs was once carried out by shepherds' boys, kids between seven and twelve years old who spent all day running circles around the flock whichever way the head shepherd ordered. Nowadays their duties are less grueling: they go from town to pasture to take shepherds their lunch, their medicine, or deliver orders from the farmers, and from the pasture back to town to tell the owners how their flocks are doing; or they gather firewood for kitchen stoves, or ferry the wine-skin from shepherd to shepherd . . . Of course, like the adults whose company they keep, they also have to endure storms, protecting themselves with goatskins (umbrellas are costly and only head shepherds can afford them). And when the flock is too far away to be herded into a sheep-fold, or the hut too small to accommodate everyone, it's the shepherds' boys who sleep out in the open, weathering the frost and dew. But that's the life of a shepherd, and as they themselves say, if you can't take it, you'd better die young.

So, like so many kids, Ramón of Casa Badiello learned the shepherds' trade by starting off as a shepherd's boy. Given that Casa Badiello is one of the poorest, and that Ramón already had older brothers who were *tiones* and tended to what little cattle and arable land they possessed, he went to work at Casa Torrera.

He began to live a shepherd's life, eating breadcrumbs fried with a scrap of bacon and potatoes as his daily meal, learning to weather the cold and sun, use slings and crooks, read the clouds and the winds. I think, deep down, he actually liked it, because it suited his restless, rebellious spirit and his love of freedom.

Occasionally, after sunset, he'd come to my house and ask to borrow a storybook, something he could read without too much trouble. I was touched, and, unaware of the future I was helping to sow, I lent him fairy tales by Grimm, by Andersen; and later, when his reading skills were more advanced, I lent him a novel or two. It's true they sometimes came back a bit damp if he got caught in a storm on the mountain and water got into his oilskin pack, but I never really minded. I was glad to have found someone who loved literature as much as I did!

My job is undoubtedly a thankless one. Typically, I don't bother to teach your average boys and girls from poor houses any more than their numbers and the few letters contained in their names, so they can sign them rather than draw a shameful x. Soon, by the time they turn seven or eight—nine if they're lucky—they're put to work at the house. Heirs are allowed a bit more education, since they have to be able to read and do basic math to keep track of the house's accounts, so they stay on at school until eleven or twelve. And finally, paradoxically, the second-born from wealthy households stay in school the longest—until they're sent off to an academy if they're going into the military or plan to have a career, or until they start at the Seminary.

Even that short, precarious education is viewed as excessive and indulgent, and it's not unusual for kids to miss class whenever help is needed at the house. And forget about giving them homework to do on Sundays, because they spend the day scouring sheep tracks in search of tufts of wool that might have gotten caught in the brush, or taking horse dung left on the trail out to their house's vegetable gardens.

So you'll understand why I felt a certain predilection for this boy who rebelled against the ignorance that was his destiny and, rather than carve boxwood spoons or figurines or sing traditional ballads in his idle time, chose instead to read. No doubt he put up with a lot of teasing. And I've now learned that everyone saw his love of reading as a sign of peculiarity, a stigma that set him apart from the rest. I even think that when I was compiling the first version of events I was obliged to transcribe, I sensed a sort of silent reproach: it's all well and good for a shepherd to be able to count so he can tell if any sheep are missing, and the fact that everyone here can sign his name lends our town a bit of prestige; but that's enough. Because any more than that and people start dreaming, wishing things were different than they are; but since things are the way they are, and cannot and must not change, then dreaming incites evil and tragedies like the one that befell us here.

At any rate, I was ignorant of all that and didn't know I

was stoking anything but a legitimate desire to learn. I had no way of knowing that he, after reading the novels of Sir Walter Scott, would think of the flocks as armies; his crook a lance; his slingshot a bow; the huts where he slept, fortresses. And I certainly had no way to predict he might dream of a fair maiden he could love and who would love him back. Had I known, I'd have felt sorrow and fear, because there are certain things that were forbidden to him by birth. But none of the books I lent him mentioned that.

I was witness to what turned out to be the spark that set off all subsequent events. It must have been shortly after New Year's Eve 1927, or maybe '28; it had snowed quite a bit and the sheep were all stabled, providing the shepherds with some very atypical free time.

I'd been invited to lunch at Casa Torrera, one of the most powerful households in town. Every heir in the province had his eye on Casa Torrera, for one exceptionally rare and important reason: there was a chance it might one day become his. That's no trifling matter, if you consider that the Casa Torrera patrimony includes six pairs of tilling mules, two yokes of oxen, over five thousand sheep, three hundred goats, ten cows, forty yokes of meadowland for making hay, fifty yokes of grain fields (ten of which are first-class, bordering the river) . . . Add to that the plentiful vineyards, the almond groves and olive trees, vegetable gardens, potato patches, hemp fields, willows, and firewood scrub, and you get an idea of how vast its holdings, and why all of the other houses took such interest.

The master of Casa Torrera is named Mariano—Mariano Banegas, in case you're curious about his surname— and the mistress, his wife: Elisa. Their marriage produced a daughter named Alba, almost the same age as Ramón.

Alba was lucky to have been born into such a wealthy family, since first-born daughters rarely survive in poorer houses, tending either to be stillborn or die the day they're delivered—providing for a daughter who will not only bring no benefit to the house but also require a dowry is very costly, you see. It's a luxury that can only be afforded if there are already a few sons to do the necessary work.

But Don Mariano could afford a daughter and then some (after all, didn't he have fifty yokes of grain fields?), and so it was that Alba came to exist.

Shortly after she was born, Don Mariano came down with the mumps. Imagine! Thirty years old and he comes down with the mumps! The whole town laughed, picturing him with his face swollen up like an acorn. When they sent one of their hands out on mule to get the doctor, we began to worry: you don't go call the doctor who lives a whole day's ride away for a simple case of mumps. Of course, Casa Torrera could afford that sort of indulgence; but given the master and mistress's tight-fistedness—identical, by the way, to that of every other master and mistress in the region—we were taken aback.

So folks laid siege to Casa Torrera, and anyone who came out was interrogated. Finally, the mystery was solved. It seems that the inflammation caused by the mumps had made its way down to his manhood, which caused him excruciating pain that was not alleviated either by cold baths or orchid roots, the traditional remedies for such ills.

The townsfolk's hilarity knew no bounds. They wrote mean-spirited ballads expounding a thousand and one theories about exactly what Don Mariano might have been doing with his private parts, and how that related to the inflammation in his mouth. At the bar, men conjectured about the size of said parts and placed more than a few substantial bets on it. And they parodied the way they imagined he might walk, with such a bulge between his legs.

How cruel—you might be thinking—to poke fun at a suffering man! But you have to understand that very few things actually happen around here; and of those very few things, even fewer are comical. So it's no surprise that when something that warrants a little revelry does come to pass, it's pounced upon, thoroughly exploited, guarded like a treasure and recounted time and again, year after year. That mule that kicked tío Anselmo so hard he flew into the trough, or the time María of Casa Simó fell headfirst from a hayloft smack into a haystack and ended up showing everyone her legs . . . and what's between them! They're silly little incidents, trivial matters, but they're some of the only lighthearted things that happen here. What else do you expect us to talk about when we go drink wine at the bar? The dark clouds threatening to pelt the crops and spread hunger throughout the village? The children that every parent has lost to typhus, to pneumonia, to scarlet fever or to we-never-found-out-what, since there was no money to call the doctor? Or whether this time the wife will die in childbirth, like so many others?

Try to understand, dear reader, that these innocent jokes, though cruel, are less so than life in the mountains; and if village women want to know every little thing you're up to, it's only because they lead empty lives; and if we make light of everything, it's only to keep from crying.

Don Mariano tried to keep the doctor's news a secret, but it was no use. It began as a quiet murmur, like a stream rising in springtime; then, as speculation was corroborated, it grew stronger; finally it just became a certainty:

Don Mariano had become sterile. Don't ask me how it could have gotten out: maybe a few incautious words were exchanged in the dining room when he and his wife thought they were alone; or perhaps they whispered something in the privacy of their own bedroom . . . Casa Torrera is enormous, as befits their station, but the walls are thin and so many people live there, what with all of the servants, maids, hands, shepherds . . .

So what the doctor had broached as a possibility, in the minds of everyone in town turned into a certainty when months passed and Elisa, Don Mariano's wife, didn't get pregnant. And since small-town minds don't see much difference between being sterile, being impotent, and being castrated, Don Mariano was christened with a spiteful nickname: the Capon, or the castrated cock. Lord knows, all and sundry had a score to settle with Casa Torrera, and no one was going to squander this opportunity.

Nicknames are a curious thing. Any silly little thing can give rise to them, but then they stick to the victim like a leech. At first, he'll put up a fight, get angry, refuse to respond when called by the name; but sooner or later, he'll have to resign himself to being known as *Moro* or *Negro* or *Blanco*, even if there's nothing in the world to justify it. And he can just thank his stars if it's not too offensive a name.

The Capon, though . . . that's real spite. When Don Mariano found out about it—the victim must always find out about it, you see, or there's no point—he was livid. That very night, he took his wife so furiously and so many times that no one at Casa Torrera slept a wink, because Don Mariano made sure to carry out the act—or acts—as raucously as possible.

All for naught. A son was the only thing that could rid

him of the name, but the son didn't come, not then or ever. And after a year, desperate and irate, he committed one of the worst crimes anyone around here can think of. He happened upon Manuela, the wife of José, master of Casa Sopena, and with hardly a word, he ravished her. As you might imagine, Casa Sopena saw this as a mortal offense, because when the next child was born, no one would know who the father was, and it's hard enough to raise a child without the added worry of whether or not it's even yours. Normally, the score would have been settled with a good thrashing for the wife and—depending on the husband's mood and valor—maybe for the guilty party, too; either that or one day at dusk a hunting rifle would be fired from the bushes.

I'm convinced that Don Mariano wouldn't have minded dying if that would have led to public recognition of his virility; but instead, people just laughed, the way they do when a wether—that's a castrated ram—tries fruitlessly to mate with a nanny goat. Even Manuela got off with no more than a couple of smacks.

Soon Don Mariano began to hound all the married women in town, daring to try it on even with those from houses as powerful as his own. What's more, he was fairly successful at it since the women talked privately among themselves at the washing place. It seems—the reader will excuse me if I'm not entirely clear about the details—they enjoyed themselves more with him than they did with their husbands, in part because they didn't fear getting pregnant, and in part because Don Mariano deemed it essential to his manhood that he take them to the heights of ecstasy repeatedly—and in order to do so employed techniques their husbands would never have condescended to use.

So among all the men in town, Don Mariano, laugh-ingly known as the Capon, came to be a pathetic, countri-fied Don Juan Tenorio of sorts. He deferred only to vir-gins, because if you deflower a virgin and can't or won't marry her, you're required to pay compensation to her house: an indemnity equivalent to the very large dowry her future husband will demand in exchange for accepting her. And in the mountains, even when a man comes unhinged, as Don Mariano did, he's not about to incur useless expense.

Once Elisa, the mistress of the house, saw that her hus-band wasn't squandering their inheritance and realized that no one was going to free her of the man with a bullet to the head, she resigned herself to reality and devoted herself to the care of their daughter and the running of the household, so neglected by her husband. But the good woman didn't do it for long because two winters later her tuberculosis worsened, taking her to the grave.

Don Mariano tried to remarry, but no one wanted to give the Capon a wife, despite how tempting his offers were. He even went so far as to rape a couple of virgins from poor houses, but their masters chose financial remuneration over allowing the girls to marry him. In the end, he reconciled himself to being a widower and hired a housekeeper to raise his daughter and look after things at home.

This home is the house where I was invited to lunch with Don Mariano (never call him the Capon unless you want to make him mad). Alba, pampered by her father, was still going to school despite the fact that she was thirteen years old, and was out playing on the patio. She was always a silent little girl, even by the standards of silent folk, but she smiled—and even laughed—easily. She was smart, a good student, and had such a pleasant voice that I always chose her to recite at our end-of-year festivities. She had a sweet face, like her mother, and a delicate jaw, unlike the square jaws of mountain folks, hardened by gnawing on weeks-old black bread, or maybe by clenching their teeth to keep from complaining about their endless woes. She was too thin for the likes of people around here, but I found her beautiful. Her green eyes reminded me of an old girlfriend of mine who . . . but that doesn't matter now. As I was saying, she was a good student, and that meant she liked to read books, especially novels. Novels like those read by Ramón the shepherd.

She was playing with the other kids her age who belonged to the house, including Ramón, because she had yet to perceive their obvious social differences and still chose playmates based on how fun and friendly they were, and not on the future position they'd hold in our tiny community.

They were playing an Aragonese game we call "Ladies and Gentlemen", though it wasn't exactly the same, since they weren't old enough to be ladies or gentlemen. Normally the game is played once a year, on the night of San Silvestre, which is New Year's Eve, and this is how it goes: the young men's names are put into one straw basket, and the young ladies' in another; then slips of paper are drawn two by two to form couples, who have to dance together that night. No doubt, the older siblings had explained it to the younger ones, and now they were imitating it in their own way, which was undoubtedly more fun: in the basket of boys' names they'd also included the names of male animals—the mule, the billy-goat, the ram—and in the girls' basket went female animals; thus, silly, outrageous couples were formed, provoking much laughter: María of Casa Mateu was to marry the tomcat and they had to chase the poor thing all around the farmyard until they could trap it and she placed a kiss upon its snout; Miguel of Casa Andrés had to kiss Morena, a slightly mangy hunting hound.

I was enjoying watching them. Then they drew lots again and Alba and Ramón came out paired up. Everyone laughed—for even at that age they realized it was a couple as absurd as María and the tom, or Miguel and Morena—and, laughingly, they pronounced them man and wife. But when the pair exchanged their kiss, something made me uneasy. Perhaps it lasted just a moment too long, or maybe their bodies drew a few inches too close.

Once they'd each gone back to their places, I noticed a strange glimmer in Ramón's eyes. I can't say whether Alba reciprocated, for I couldn't see her eyes from where I was sitting. But before I had time to see anything else we were called to lunch and off we went, Alba and I to the dining room, the others either back home or—in the case of Ramón and the other servant kids—to the basement, where they ate.

Early the next day, well before dawn, there came a knock at my door. I opened it up and there stood Ramón, wrapped in his goatskin, birch gaiters covering his shins so the snow wouldn't soak his socks.

He claimed he was returning newspapers. Lately I'd begun lending him the paper after I'd finished reading it so that he could learn what was going on in the world, even though there was little chance of any outside event actually affecting his life; still, I lent the papers on the condition that when he finished, he return them to me, because they worked well for lighting the hearth or keeping my chest warm.

Needless to say, that didn't merit such an early visit. I lit a candle so we could see, since the lamp oil I'd bought the year before was almost gone and I wouldn't be able to buy more until the following month. Then I asked him what he wanted.

He rubbed his legs a little, cleared his throat, looked every which way, and finally asked:

"What can I do to earn a whole lot of money?"

When a thirteen-year-old kid wakes you up in the middle of the night—I don't know what time it was, but it was very early—and asks you a question like that, it's hard to give a good answer. In fact, it's hard to give a good answer anytime: after all, if I knew the answer, what on earth would I be doing here in this godforsaken town? So I chose to reply with a question of my own.

"What do you want to earn a whole lot of money for?"

"So I can marry Alba from Casa Torrera."

So it hadn't been my imagination! I had to smile, seeing a boy entertain such thoughts. Nevertheless, for a minute, I saw clearly how cruel Ramón's lot in life was: all those dreams, for nothing! He'd herd sheep for the rest of his life and was never going to earn enough to support a wife—and I don't mean Alba, because even a second-born girl from a poor house was entirely out of his reach, at least until he became head shepherd. Yes, he'd make it to head shepherd, because he was strong and smart, but not before he turned fifty; no one entrusted the herd to anyone younger than that; and by that time he wouldn't be able to start a family, since not long after that his strength would wane and he'd have to donate himself to the same house he'd worked at his entire life.

And Alba? Not a chance. Ever since her father had

gone from being Don Mariano to the Capon, all the strong houses had been wangling to have their heir marry her. It was an exceptional opportunity. Rather than demand a dowry, as is the custom, they were now offering her father their best fields, their strongest pairs of mules, the huts providing the best shelter . . . Nothing was too much, provided it knocked the rival house out of the competition. The masters, normally so acquisitive, now made reckless offers, because, after all, it would all come back to them as part of the inheritance. What chance did Ramón have, even if he did earn a lot of money? No, even if he got her pregnant, they'd force her to drink meadow-rue tea to induce a miscarriage, or the baby would die in childbirth, or be left in a foundling hospital; and then Alba would marry whomever her father chose. There was too much at stake for anyone to care about the girl's virtue.

"As long as her father is alive," I said to Ramón, "you will never be allowed to marry Alba."

He stood thoughtfully for a moment, and then asked:

"What if he died?"

That startled me.

"Why would he die? He's young and strong, he's healthy, has no diseases and he's not going hungry." And to myself, I added, "and it seems no one is going to do anything to put a stop to his lechery."

"The problem," I went on, "is that you'll never have as much money, or land, or cattle as the powerful houses; and it's only natural for her father to want to give her away to the richest man, since he's in a position to choose."

"That's not fair!" he cried bitterly. "How come the masters and the heirs get to have all that money, and land, and cattle, and sleep in beds, and eat what they want, and get married? I know how to read, too, and I can count every sheep in a flock, not like other shepherds who have to use a stone every time they get to fifty. I've read books that heirs have never even heard of!"

I let out a sigh. Asking these kinds of questions was exactly what had truncated my career to begin with, banished me to a town the whole world was oblivious to. That a poor shepherd might also ask them was not a good sign.

"What if I left, went far away, to Zaragoza, or Barcelona, or America? I can read and write and multiply—well, sometimes I make mistakes—, and I know about Stalin and Mussolini and García-Prieto, and a lot of other people they talk about in the newspaper. I bet I could make a lot of money there, a lot more than working as a shepherd!"

How could I explain to a boy just on the brink of manhood that making money requires more than knowing how to read and write and multiply, even if you *don't* make mistakes? How could I explain about factories where people work twelve or fourteen hours a day, about workers' slums wiped out by typhus, about mining disasters? And how could I explain that although it might seem to him that those workers earned a fortune, they then had to buy food, since their masters didn't feed them, and pay rent, and buy clothes and tram fare? How could he grasp that when a worker gets old he can't donate himself to his master and if he has no children to take him in, he simply sinks into destitution? No, I couldn't tell him anything, except that if he left he wouldn't earn as much money as he thought; and above all that if he left, when he came back, Alba would surely have married someone else.

Dejected, he returned to work. He had to feed the sheep hay, since the ground was covered in snow and they couldn't graze. I went back to bed, so as not to waste any more candles, and tried, with no luck, to sleep despite the fact that I kept telling myself: He's just being a boy! He'll forget about her! Perhaps, deep in my heart, I already knew it wasn't so.

CHAPTER IV

We never brought the matter up again, and if I didn't know Ramón so well I'd have said that he'd forgotten all about his childish love. But there was something about the dogged way he worked, the single-mindedness with which he read, the math equations he worked on, the fiery determination in his eyes, that told me that his heart still beat for Alba.

Most men work just to survive, without ever really questioning the point of our existence, and we go about our work honestly, if not ardently. Others work out of greed, for though they have enough to get by, they crave more so they can outclass the neighbors, add land to their patrimony, prove to themselves that they're better than the rest, acquire power or honor, and pretend—in vain—that they won't one day simply turn to dust; these are the men and women who build factories, erect cities, govern states.

And then there's a special class of men who, in the deepest part of their souls, feel a restlessness they can't contain. A drunkenness of sorts seems to pacify them, but it also hones their insights; and a force more powerful than social convention and prudent judgment leads them to do crazy things. These are the kind of men who rile the world, or save it; who unleash revolutions, or violently suppress them; who produce great works of art, or destroy them. If they die for what springs from their souls, they'll be seen as martyrs, or saints, or mystics; if they kill for it, they'll be terrorists, conquerors or dictators. I'm afraid that Ramón, the silent little blue-eyed boy shepherd, was this kind of man, and though I'm sure that in his dreams he was willing to die for his love, his daily struggle to survive made it much more likely that he'd fight mercilessly for it.

Don't get me wrong. I am not, like the rest of town, endorsing the idea that Ramón was wicked from the start. Not at all. Unlike those from theplains, men from these parts—tough, hardy mountain men—fight the hostile, inhospitable forces of nature from the day they're born. Here, every bushel of wheat has to be wrenched from the land with sweat; fields must be cleared year after year; the mountains that protect us and produce our meadows also bring storms and squalls. And of all the mountain men, the toughest are the shepherds. They are the ones who have to walk all day along narrow paths, scratched by thorns, stand up to wolves and vipers, brave therains without abandoning their posts . . . Give them a flag to fight for and they'll become ferocious soldiers ready to invade the valley to conquer Moorish cities; show them a far-off continent where they can escape poverty, and they'll annihilate ancient civilizations. But for now they tend the flocks, and anyone who doesn't know them might mistake their capacity to withstand pain for resignation, or their patience in waiting to seek revenge for meekness.

Now Ramón had a flag to follow, a heaven to get to; and while he might fight for it, any of his fellow shepherds would have been just as determined and tenacious.

A short time later, Ramón was promoted to third shepherd, and so, no longer performing the duties of a shepherd's boy, he began earning a few pesetas each year.

Normally, shepherds are chosen at the Feria de San Miguel, at the end of September; and as part of the deal, which is almost always oral, it's agreed that the rancher will feed and lodge the shepherd as per our custom, and provide the necessary tools and clothes: sandals, a knife, a blanket . . . As and when a shepherd needs supplies over the course of the year, the master provides them and makes note of how much they cost, and then subtracts the amount from his wages; he'll also take off for any days the shepherd was sick and any sheep that, in his estimation, were lost due to the shepherd's negligence. So occasionally it turns out that, rather than earn money, the shepherd actually ends up owing it.

Ramón subjected himself to a Spartan routine, even from a shepherd's perspective. He didn't take up smoking, the way almost all the rest did, despite the other shepherds' teasing; and I knew that it was in order not to spend the few pesetas on the terrible-quality cut tobacco they rolled. Nor did he swig *vinada*, the awful drink that shepherds procured from the macerated remains of the last wine pressing. Not only that, but he went barefoot except in winter, so as to save a bit of money and not wear out his sandals. And though he might be sick, he'd never send to the pharmacy for medicine, instead using the plants that shepherds know so well—plantain for eyes and abrasions, spruce blossom for colds and festering wounds, oak for summertime diarrhea, bramble for sore throats—and preparing remedies himself. And needless to say, he never visited prostitutes, much to the other shepherds' astonishment.

The others looked at him and said, "He's cooking some-thing up!" but couldn't imagine, even remotely, what it was. The fact that he didn't like going with women, didn't enjoy betting a few cents on cards . . . No, it just wasn't normal: and what about the whole reading business? That really is the limit! When Ramón has free time, rather than talk about animals, about whether those clouds bode well or ill, about the season's weather so far, or about girls' hips and breasts, he opens his pouch and takes out the news-papers that the teacher lends him and reads nonsense about cities as far away as Barcelona and Madrid, maybe even farther.

Despite the endless ways they tried, they were never able to wheedle out of him what he was saving his money for. At the end of the first year, Ramón had enough to buy three "feeble" sheep. Don't ask me how you can tell the difference between a "feeble" sheep and a normal one, or even a good one. I know it's easy for a shepherd, but to me—what can I say?—a sheep is a sheep, end of story.

Well it seems that Ramón pampered his three sheep, which owing to ancient custom had the right to graze with his master's flock. He'd pull up clumps of fresh, tender grass from gulleys for them to eat—though never when it was wet, because that could lead to bloating and kill them; give them ash twigs in wintertime; clean even the tiniest of sores with juniper oil to keep flies from depositing larvae in them . . . So, after a year of his care, the three "feeble" sheep had become "regular" sheep and given birth to four lambs: one male and three female. He kept the females and sold the male, and thus, when his master paid him the following year, he was able to buy three more sheep: two feeble and one good one.

Season after season, making a thousand sacrifices, he slowly built up his own flock. And after four years he had over twenty of his own sheep, which was incredible for such a young shepherd. I was his only confidant. We didn't talk about what lay behind all his efforts: in that, his modesty and shyness were absolute; maybe he was afraid I would point out that his dream was unattainable.

We didn't talk about his objective, either, aside from that of owning more and more sheep. I didn't want to discourage him by asking how many he thought he'd need in order to buy—yes, I think buy is just the word—his true love. A thousand? Two thousand? How long would she remain unwed? She was already seventeen and if she hadn't married yet, it was only because month after month her father saw the offers multiply and couldn't bring himself to pick one, knowing that soon an even better one would come along. But it wouldn't be long now.

No, the only thing he talked to me about was sheep: this one looks like she's going to have twins. Or, this one looks sick, she might have worms in her gut; I'd better give her a purgative. And I can still recall how frantic he was when one of them got the staggers and stumbled around in a circle after none of the remedies he knew—be they plants, prayers or magic—had any effect. Everyone says he wept when he had to kill her; I didn't see it myself, but tears were shed when he told me about it later, just as they were when one of his feeble sheep died one winter despite his ministrations.

We did speak a bit about what we read in Don Casildo's papers, and I'd go over his accounts (he was pretty good at division). Other times, we'd just sit in silence, staring into the fire.

Alba kept growing, both in stature and in beauty, and she stopped coming to class in order to devote her time to the chores that even rich heiresses are required to do in these wretched hills. She never confided in me, who knows why; perhaps she was more discrete than Ramón. At any rate, I can't say much about the girl: if it weren't for Ramón confiding in me, I would never have guessed that behind her meek, docile look was a burning love—or passion, if you prefer—and that she, too, was capable of defying the world, not violently, but with the deliberate obstinacy of an old oak whose roots eventually break through stone. To me, her old teacher, she still seemed like a little girl.

One summer day, the very thing I knew would one day happen, happened. It was inevitable; there's just no way to keep secrets in a house. Her father, the Capon (sorry, I mean Don Mariano) caught wind of what was going on. How did he find out about it? Did he himself see looks exchanged, glimpse an imprudent expression, a reckless gesture? Or did someone from the house betray them? It makes no difference!

Don Mariano was no fool—despite his obsession with proving his virility—and around here if you're going to take revenge, you do it well or you don't do it at all. A less shrewd father would have flown into a rage and kicked out the miserable shepherd who'd dared lay eyes—and who knows what else—on his daughter and his inheritance, and the whole town would have had something to laugh and gossip about. Then, his daughter's worth would have shrunk a tad; not much, though, because what folks found most attractive about her was her inheritance, not her virtue.

Not Don Mariano, though. His response was to be so

devastating that no one in town would dare laugh; everyone would see that with him, you had to watch your step. Jokes would be replaced by fear. He kept his mouth shut, and the only thing that betrayed the fact that he was up to anything at all was his not going out as often in search of adventure. Apart from that, he kept his eyes and ears open, put a woman he trusted in charge of his daughter, and waited.

The Feria de San Miguel, which as I said is celebrated at the end of September, is very popular among folks living in farming towns. People bring to the plaza the cattle they want to sell, artisans display their cowbells—small and large—and collars; shepherds publicly renew contracts with their masters, all in an atmosphere of high-spirited revelry that usually ends at night with a dance to celebrate the profitable deals that everyone—from the biggest to the smallest—has made.

Don Mariano asked Ramón to take a few sheep to the plaza to sell, and he obeyed without suspecting a thing. I saw him there and chatted a bit with him about this and that while his master haggled with a dealer. Then, Don Mariano turned to Ramón with a casual air, and spat out:

"By the way, I want you to know that I'm not renewing your contract. Take the day's wages I owe you; you can look for a new master today, but tomorrow you'll have to leave the house, and take your sheep with you."

And if you can believe it, he said all this with a smile on his face! He didn't even raise his voice. Then, calmly, he went over to look at some little sheep bells being sold by a traveling salesman, a gypsy people knew from other fairs.

Needless to say, the color drained from Ramón's face. Renewing contracts at the Feria de San Miguel is more a ritual than an actual renewal, because firing a shepherd is almost unheard of, something done only in cases of utter ineptitude. This was a true insult. But since Ramón could read the many silences of hill talk, he knew why he was being fired, though he had yet to figure out how far-reaching Don Mariano's deviousness would turn out to be. He thought he'd be able to find another master, not realizing that over the past several days, Don Mariano had visited every one of the powerful houses in town to keep that from happening, threatening never to give them his daughter, to forbid their cattle to pass through his land, or simply to consider them enemies.

No one is about to pit themselves against a rich house over one miserable little shepherd, with so many of them to go around; and they also didn't want to hire anyone so bold as to chase after a house's daughter. And for heaven's sake, shepherds can't be allowed to forget who they are and where they stand; if that were tolerated, they'd get bold and cocky.

Ramón offered his services to every rancher sauntering around the plaza, Don Mariano's sardonic eye looking on all the while as he continued to feign great interest in the gypsy merchant's bells. My friend was like a leper, turned away by all, or maybe a ghost who roams the world, invisible to men. When he passed by, their conversation would grow animated, more animated than ever in fact, to conceal their embarrassment. They went on discussing whether a certain yearling had been mounted, whether that mule had gotten all of its teeth in yet, or anything else they could think of; and they pretended not to sense Ramón's presence. When he finally gathered up enough courage to interrupt them, asking if they needed his services, they'd turn as if they had only just noticed him standing there, and then rebuff him with the same gesture they would have used to shoo an especially irritating cloud of flies. Then they resumed their conversation, irked at the inopportune distraction.

After he'd approached the last rancher, he began offering himself to poor houses at laughable prices, no longer aiming for a shepherd's post and now willing to accept any miserable job: building stone walls, clearing fields, chopping wood . . . These men hadn't been paid a visit by Don Mariano, because they're not important enough, but they know which way the wind blows, and no one dared offer him even the most menial odd job.

Finally, he stood stock still like a post, in the middle of the plaza, staring into space, his face furrowed by streaming tears he was unable to hold back. He, who over the years had undergone a thousand hardships for love, was weeping. And everyone pretended not to see him. Don Mariano ignored him with mocking superiority; the ranchers and powerful landowners couldn't help but smile on seeing his humiliation—he, the boy bold enough to challenge them; the small landholders let out a sigh of relief, thankful that they themselves didn't have to sell their labor power to the higher-ups, not realizing that they too were subjected to their designs and demeaned themselves before them; the peons, shepherds, serfs, *tiones* and all those who, in general, possessed nothing but their own strength, looked down and felt a sense of shame that their simple minds couldn't quite comprehend. Everyone, whether out of hate or fear, turned their back on him.

And what about me, you must be asking? Had we not, over the course of all those years, built up a solid friendship? Had I not harbored the hope that, against all reason, he would manage to raise himself from the place where fate had cast him? Why did I not go to him, put my hand on his shoulder?

I'm no coward; don't think poorly of me. I, too, had ideals, and I fought for them. In 1909 I was teaching at Ferrer y Guardia Modern School. And although everyone knows that the famous educator Ferrer y Guardia was unjustly killed by a government firing squad in retaliation for the events of Semana Trágica, the tragic week, and that the schools which applied his pedagogy were shut down, no one thinks about what happened to us poor teachers. Jobless, rejected by everyone, we were forced into a domestic exile of sorts, forced to move to towns as poor and isolated as this one.

At first I dreamed of going back to Barcelona, strolling down the Ramblas, seeing my friends, and putting the world to right over long discussions in cafés; and I hated these inhospitable mountains and cold stone houses, these people with weather-beaten faces and hearts of steel. But everything dies eventually, even hope; and my rage slowly gave way to resignation.

When the Republic was formed, I could have returned to Barcelona, but what was I going to do there? My friends, no doubt, had long since forgotten me, and I don't even know where my relatives live. Besides, I'm over fifty now; too old to marry, and soon I'll be too old to work.

I see myself as an old village schoolteacher who, when he's too rickety to continue holding class, will be taken in by alternating houses in exchange for taking care of a child, sweeping the patio or any menial little chore an old man can do. And would you honestly expect me to exchange an old age like that for some lonely hovel in a city where no one knows me, for a pension that doesn't even pay enough to survive?

No, I'm no coward, but nor am I a hero. Ramón was now a leper, stigmatized, a foreign body being expelled from the heart of the community; and his leprosy would have extended to anyone who dared come near him. And I, as I've already said, am over fifty years old and rely for my sustenance on the good will of the people. No, I'm no coward, please don't think that . . . but I am over fifty.

So Ramón was all alone, abandoned by everyone. He could have gone back to the house where he was born— Casa Badiello—and turned over his twenty sheep and the money he'd earned that year to the common fund, and become a disinherited *tión* like so many others. But that would have meant admitting his defeat, renouncing forever his dream of marrying Alba; and the townspeople, appeased by this triumph of reason and good order, would have forgiven him, and accepted the repentant prodigal son back into the their fold.

But instead, Ramón went back to Casa Torrera, tossed into his satchel a loaf of bread and a few miserable belongings—his frying pan, knife, lighter, shaving implements, etc.—donned his goatskin and blanket and, picking up his crook, took his sheep and headed for the sierra's communal pastures. It was clear that no one was going to rent him out any of the valley's winter meadows, and he refused to trample his dignity any further by begging in vain.

I watched him head off alone, leading his miserable flock, not a single friendly hand held up to him in farewell not a single voice wishing him bon voyage or good luck.

I bit my lip in rage and impotence. Watching Ramón

disappear down the mountain path, I couldn't help but recall that the merenderas, those little purple flowers with delicious bulbs that sprout up from the ground, were already beginning to bloom. And I was thinking it because everyone says that when the merenderas come out, it's time for shepherds to head back to the valley so the snow doesn't take them by surprise.

I looked up at the autumn sky and deplored the approaching winter.

CHAPTER V

Nature is generous in the autumn, as if asking forgiveness for the cold to come. Not only could Ramón eat the snakes, lizards, frogs and locusts he caught, he could also pull trout from the streams with his bare hands and trap rabbits. In addition to the merendera I mentioned, the vegetable kingdom provided a supply of bitter but nourishing dandelions, acidic sorrel, buried orchid bulbs, sweet burdock roots, delicate marshmallow flowers, and delicious nettles that lose all their sting once they've been cooked. Nor was there any dearth of fruit: blackberries from the tangled bramble bushes, raspberries sweet as candy, tiny wild strawberries, black gooseberries, bitter sloe berries, buttery elderberries, dog rose hips whose seeds and fuzz had to be carefully removed . . . not to mention nutritious hazelnuts, beechnuts, and acorns. And with the first rains came a plethora of edible fungi that appeared on the meadows and in the forests: boletes, fairy rings, milk-caps, morels, rat's foot, lichens . . . Since he'd grown up foraging in the mountains for things to supplement his dreary, monotonous diet of breadcrumbs fried with bacon—which he ate almost every day—there was no danger of Ramón mistaking the similar taste and appearance of toxic belladonna for redoul, or taking poisonous colchium for sweet merendera, or confusing fly-agaric or gray pinkgill with some other mushroom.

It was like a misleading trip through the Garden of Eden, back when men didn't have to sweat to earn their living; but Ramón was well aware that the abundance was a mirage and that with the first snows, survival would be near impossible if he didn't hoard enough food for himself and his poor flock.

Like a man possessed, he devoted himself feverishly to stockpiling provisions in a cave—well, rather than an actual cave, it was a recess in a south-facing wall sometimes used in the summer to shelter sheep at night. Using dogwood branches, he wove primitive baskets, which he filled with beechnuts, hazelnuts and acorns, and then hung from the roof to keep rats from making off with them; he set forest fruits out to dry—the ones he thought would lend themselves to it—, intuiting that they contained substances essential to his survival; using the stalks from the nettles he ate, he made rope for stringing mushrooms out to dry; he smoked some trout, splitting them open and gutting them with sticks, although he didn't have enough salt to cure them and couldn't expect them to last . . .

In addition to preparing food, he also amassed pinecones and candles so he could light a fire; and since he had no axe, he collected firewood from fallen trees as best he could. He also made himself a bed of dried leaves and grass. And, on rainy days when he couldn't go out to forage, he built walls out of reeds and mud to protect his little abode from the wind.

But Ramón didn't think only of himself. He also used a primitive sickle he'd carved from boxwood to cut tall grass from the streambeds and pile it up near his cave, making a haystack. He hacked down large numbers of ash branches, since that way their leaves would retain all of their nutritional value, and created a good place for his sheep to sleep in his cave, too, so they could stay warm.

He worked tirelessly, hardly stopping to sleep, because he knew that every second, every ounce of food or heat, might be decisive.

When a few of the shepherds from Casa Bardal came back to town with the news that they'd seen him hauling sacks of acorns, and then others said that Ramón was piling firewood up in the Moor's Cave, we realized that he was determined to hold out through the winter. Or else to die, if he failed.

As if Ramón had suddenly earned everyone's respect, that fall the shepherds didn't cut ash, the kids didn't hunt wild forest fruits like they did every year, and the old folks didn't pass the time foraging for mushrooms. By tacit agreement, the mountain belonged to Ramón: the shepherds explained to their masters that since he'd been banished by the people, at least he had a right to the gifts provided by God. The masters ground their teeth in rage when their shepherds told them that taking the herd up to the sierra to finish off the remaining blades of grass would be a sin. It's not that we want to disobey you, God forbid, we would never do that, but the Lord would punish us, lightning might strike the flock and kill the sheep; sure, there's always a black sheep to protect us from thunderstorms, but God is stronger than black sheep; but we're not disobeying you, no sir, it's just that we can't graze the flock up there.

That was an exceptionally hard winter, or perhaps it

seemed that way to us because we knew what Ramón was going through. For the first time since I'd lived there, the town was riven by hatred. On one side, the big ranchers and the masters of the smaller houses: they felt as if the presence of that wretched young man was a threat to the established order, in place since time immemorial; and when they looked to the snow-capped sierra—we all looked to the sierra quite often in those days—it was as though they foresaw the danger emanating from it, a lethal plague that they had no idea how to fight.

On the other side, the *tiones*, shepherds, peons, servants—in a word, all those who would never own property, who would only ever earn just enough to feed themselves—looked up at the sierra in admiration. They would never venture to do anything like that themselves, but there was someone up there brave enough to defy his destiny, someone like them who wouldn't give in and who was fighting to defend his right to love. And so they forgave him his strange habit of reading, and his proverbial stinginess, and his talents and skills, because now they saw that it was all in the name of achieving a single goal: to be worthy of marrying the woman he loved; and for that they respected him like no one else. It was as though they wanted to live, through Ramón, what they themselves would never live, and they prayed for the Virgen de la Piedad and San Andrés and San Miguel to perform a miracle that would allow Ramón to marry Alba, and have land, and cattle, and children.

But since neither the Virgen de la Piedad nor San Andrés nor San Miguel performed any such miracle, the dispossessed felt their oppression weighing down upon them as never before, and they despised their masters for it.

That year, wolves ate sheep, rats gnawed at the wheat stored in barns, and the wind blew away the haystacks. Nothing out of the ordinary, these things happen all the time, but this time the masters could have sworn that part of what was lost ended up in the Moor's Cave. They couldn't prove it, though, despite interrogating their head-shepherds and servants insistently: no one knew a thing. And the chasm of mistrust grew wider.

Occasionally, a group of hunters chasing a wild boar—taking advantage of their forced winter leisure time—caught a glimpse of Ramón with his sheep, for he grazed them in the forests where the snow wasn't as deep and they could always chomp something off of low-hanging branches. No doubt he was on occasion within rifle range, and more than one of them must have thought about shooting him and then claiming it was a hunting accident; but they never dared.

Perhaps it's also occurred to you that nothing would have been easier than heading up to the Moor's Cave one night and shooting an unarmed man; folks have been shot for much less, especially during these troubled times we live in. But as I've said, mountain folks—masters and servants alike—are smart. Ramón had become a symbol, and if they'd killed him, the hatred of the oppressed would have been uncontainable, and sooner or later would have surged up to overthrow the system. No, Ramón had to be broken, humiliated, vanquished. He'd get tired of holding out in the sierra, and besides, Alba would marry an heir soon; she was already eighteen, which is getting to be late for marriage. And after all, from up in the sierra, there was nothing he could do to stop it.

I only managed to see Alba on the few occasions when

her father invited me to lunch or when she came down—always with an escort—to the washing place or the fountain. She was always quiet, never said a word, her eyes downcast so that no one could see how red they were, her pallor like that of her mother, who had died of tuberculosis. Perhaps in the city she could have been considered a beauty, for she was delicate and had a sensitive, romantic air about her, and it wasn't just her face and body that made you feel nostalgic, and flustered; her gestures, her gaze, even the tone of her voice made you want to surrender, stretching out your arms to her in a spontaneous, protective embrace. But beneath her tearful eyes lay a tenacious resolve akin to Ramón's.

Here, in these harsh environs, however, people considered her body too delicate. The ideal of beauty in this part of the world consists of wide hips made for bearing children, an ample bosom to feed them, strong shoulders to work the land, and a portly body to warm the bed at night; as you can see, it's all very utilitarian, and left not a glimmer of hope for Alba's poetic soul.

The fact that her mother, Elisa, never conformed to the ideal of mountain beauty had been a significant obstacle when it came to marrying her to an heir: no one wanted such a weak woman for a wife. But the master of Casa Torrera, Mariano's father, proved himself to be smarter than the rest, because he figured that the puny girl whose family was willing to pay an exceptionally high dowry wouldn't make it through more than one or two childbirths; then, after pocketing the dowry, Mariano would marry another woman more suited to running a household. Who could have predicted that Don Mariano would become "the Capon" and have no other descendents?

If Alba hadn't been a rich heiress, no one would have given her a second glance, with the exception of some day-dreaming young shepherd; but now her frailty did nothing but incite the greed of her potential husbands, because the sooner she died, the sooner she'd leave her husband master of two houses that, when united, would form the most powerful house in town.

Don Mariano loved his only daughter, even more so once he realized there would be no other heirs; but he loved her with a primitive, animal love: let no one try to hurt her! But it's one thing to love your daughter and quite another to miss out on the attractive offers from her suitors, all because of the whims of a young girl. Love: foolishness! Having a rich husband is what matters, a husband who doesn't get drunk too often, only beats her when she deserves it, is discreet if he goes with other women, and does so without putting the estate at risk. That's what all the girls dream of, so why should Alba be any different?

That was Don Mariano's reasoning, and he lurched from incomprehension to self-reproach: I've spoiled her, that's why she's turned out this way. I let her go to school for too long, that's where all of this is coming from. I should have been stricter with her, I know it; why, I even bought her Persil to wash with instead of the tallow-and-soda soap other women use. And the jug she takes to the fountain, isn't it metal rather than clay, so it's not too heavy for her? And if she gets tired after just a few hours of gathering sheaves, don't I let her rest? And don't I send her on errands when we're doing the hard work? People are right when they say that laziness is the mother of all vice! But then again, she's so frail! That's it; it's decided: when she marries, it's on the condition that she not be made to work too hard and do only light chores. And who can I marry her to? There's Joaquín, the heir of Casa Sosas, offering nothing less than the Quixarel windmill! And besides, a lot of the Casa Sosas land borders ours. But of course, there's also Pedro, the heir of Casa Bardají . . . Still, first I've got to get this shepherd business taken care of. Yes, well it's a good thing measures have been taken, or God only knows what might have happened.

Since Alba never spoke to anyone, Don Mariano had taken to mumbling at the table, engaging in incessant monologues that he conducted with no regard for the incidental presence of strangers like me. And while he sat there spewing that sort of blather, I looked at Alba and wanted to cry. She never should have been born there; she ought to have been a princess—everything about her revealed an uncommon sensitivity too delicate for such harsh environs. Maybe that's why she loved Ramón, though of course no one would have called Ramón delicate—he was as tough as the leather he wore—but if Alba's green eyes shone with the same steely resolve as her beloved shepherd's, his blue eyes also betrayed a sensitivity identical to hers. It was as if they said, "Let me rest, inclement nature, let my head rest in the lap of my love for just a moment, and I'll whisper poetry, weave dreams, sing love songs. If the men and the mountains would let me, in the arms of the one I love I'd learn to be soft and gentle . . ."

As you can see, I too became delirious looking at Alba and the trembling lips she pressed together in an attempt to stifle her cries as we listened to her father's deranged logic; and I felt a terrible urge to be twenty again, to not depend on being invited to lunch, to smash everything, to take her in my arms and deliver her to the one who'd make her happy, to . . . And at that moment it hit me: I'm just the old teacher at a forgotten school in a town no one's heard of; and I felt sad and pathetic, and had to wipe away a tear that was trying to escape.

Since I never interrupted Don Mariano's monologues, he found my presence more and more agreeable, forgetting that he'd initially spurned me for having taught his daughter's wretched seducer to read so well; and so it was that his invitations grew more frequent. A thousand times, in my presence, he whispered the name of every piece of property owned by every suitor, unable to make up his mind. A thousand times he hatched plans to force Ramón to leave town and move elsewhere; he even considered having Señora Teresa, the witch, cast a spell that would kill his twenty sheep, but then he reasoned that if Ramón could survive with so few sheep, he could also get by with none, and there was no sense wasting money on Señora Teresa if it wasn't even going to improve the situation.

Alba kept quiet, challenging her father's authority with a forest-like silence. It was a terrible silence.

Each morning when I woke, I went to look up at the sierra, and on clear days you could see a faint column of smoke wafting up from his fire, silhouetted against the snow. But other days, storms came along and I had no news of him, and that left me, and the rest of town, uneasy until there came another clear day and we could see that feeble plume of smoke, which for the humble was akin to the cloud Yahweh used to guide the Israelites through the desert.

At night when the wind howled at my door and the snow banged against my shutters, I thought of Ramón and couldn't sleep. I wondered what he was doing. Pressing the stones he heated in the fire against his body, perhaps? Or maybe, in a desperate attempt to find warmth, he'd burrow a hole in the ground, fill it with embers and lie on top of it, after covering it with a thin layer of sand. Or, casting off the few remaining vestiges of human dignity, did he nuzzle up against the sheep in search of body heat? Or curl up by the fire, treasuring the memory of his beloved as he tried not to use up what little firewood he had left? There were some days when, having run out of provisions, he had to insert a reed into the sebum of his best sheep to suck out their fat without having to kill them; or, when they got too thin for that, had to slice into their jugulars and drink their blood, and then stanch the flow with ash. But when spring arrived he was still alive. Emaciated, filthy, his hands and feet frost-bitten, with a wild look that was almost frightening; but alive. Ramón had managed to survive the winter thanks to his desperate resolve, his tireless work, and the help of the other shepherds.

Still, he himself knew that this purely physical endurance was never going to earn him his beloved. Winter had passed, the screech owls and tawny owls were hooting at night, and soon the cuckoo would announce the arrival of spring. Ramón, emerging from the snow, decided to put into action the plan he'd hatched during those endless nights of pain. He'd proved to all the masters that he could hold out. Now it was time to leave the mountain.

As soon as the passes were clear, he brushed the frost off his shoulders in what had become a mechanical, everyday gesture, and led his fifteen surviving sheep to the market of a nearby town, where he sold them to a trader. With what he got for the sheep and the money he'd saved like a treasure from the previous year, he bought an old mule that limped a bit but could still walk; some worn but serviceable saddles that wouldn't chafe the animal; and an ancient hunting shotgun, one of those single-shot muzzleloaders where you have to first load the powder, then the wadding and then the bullet. And with the money left over, he bought a big sword-like knife, one of those they call *facas*, to replace his shepherd's knife.

Thus outfitted, he returned to town.

CHAPTER VI

He's hardly set foot inside the municipal boundaries of Biescas de Obago when every one of its inhabitants knows that Ramón, of Casa Badiello, the man who dares stand up to the powerful, is coming back armed with a shotgun. The first shepherds to see him entrust their flocks to the inexpert watch of their shepherd boys and run to tell the others. Soon the cries, whistles, kids running barefoot, women . . . all carry the same message: Ramon's coming! And he's armed!

The whole town is overcome by a sort of delirious frenzy, overwhelming everyone's immense common sense and negligible logic. The colliers leave their miserable mud and thatch cabins, so the oak and ilex pyres go unlit; the farmhands abandon their beasts and plows halfway through a furrow. The beekeepers—there are no "apiarists" around here—leave their mud, straw and dung hives without thinking about whether there might be a swarm or not; the woodcutters stop their rhythmic chopping before the tree is felled; everyone runs to town, overtaken by reckless frenzy. And in their hands, without really knowing why, they clutch anything that might serve as a weapon: axes, canes, sickles . . .

This wave of insanity spreads to the town as well, and the carpenter neglects the wheel he was warping and takes up a gouge; the mason lets the mortar harden on the mortarboard; the farrier stops mid-task, leaving a horse shod with only four nails; furriers, rope-makers, potters, the miller, the baker . . . they all suffer from the same contagious disease that makes them desert their workplace and take up arms.

Even I felt its effects. When the apprentice cooper poked his head through the classroom window to shout that Ramón was coming down the prairie road with a shotgun, I, too, got the jitters and ran home in search of something—I didn't know what—with no concern for the schoolchildren who, in turn, sensed the magnitude of the event and ran through the streets spreading the news all over town.

I didn't know what I was looking for until I found myself with a kitchen knife in my pocket, and in my hand the cane I use when rheumatism racks my lower back. Then, having satisfied the devil who'd gotten into me, I set off to find Ramón.

I met many others on my way, and I realized that the rage and hatred we'd stored up over the winter was boiling over, not just in me but in everyone. The fact that Ramón was coming back armed was like the spark that sets the barn on fire, the sign we'd been waiting for to rise up against our fate.

Because I felt hatred—intense, irrational hatred. I hated the chilblains that plague me in the winter, the lice that take root in my scalp even though I soak my head in water steeped with cigarette butts each month, the fleas and ticks that leave bloodstains on my sheets at night, the little mice scurrying through my kitchen, the smoke from the hearth that burns my eyes, the bacon-fried breadcrumbs

I have to eat when no one invites me to lunch, the ever unfulfilled longing for a woman, the cold that never leaves me in the dark months, the veiled smugness of the landowners . . . and, like me, accompanying me in my hatred, were the others: workers, *tiones*, shepherds, farmhands . . . they too were filled with hate for the hard life that was their lot, they too wanted linen—rather than sackcloth—underclothes to keep their skin from chafing, and to eat meat once or twice a week, and to work no more than twelve or thirteen hours a day, and not to sleep seven or eight to a haystack. Without realizing it, all winter long we'd let the hatred in our souls fester; now it was overflowing in a frenzied excitement that had something sensual about it.

Because the symbol, the epitome, of our desire to change our way of life was a woman. I think we all felt the imperious need to be held, to be loved, to be consoled. We wanted to have children and a lover in our beds; and we were rising up against the cruel fate condemning us to sterility. We didn't care that our land, already overpopulated given how poor it was, could support no more families, nor that society had gone on this way, unchanged, for a thousand years; all we wanted was a woman.

And given that even the most hot-headed among us saw that the dreams we cherished deep in our souls were unrealizable and utopian, and that they'd never be fulfilled, we wanted for at least one of us to attain them. We wanted a shepherd to marry an heiress, and eat well, and not be cold in the winter. That's all. Then we'd all go back to our fields and our flocks and our forests, to our schools and workshops, reconciled to our fate. Because when Ramón held Alba in his arms, it would be us who held her, too; and she was a real woman, a wife, not a mercenary like Pilar and Jacinta. And her children would be our children; her food, our food.

Let them wed and we'd all hold out hope that a better life was possible.

As Ramón approached town, we joined him, a pack of silent men. And if there was one thing about it that made an impression me, it was the silence. In my younger days, in Barcelona, I had taken part in demonstrations, and in all of them the most notable thing was the noise, as if we had to egg each other on in order to pluck up our courage. But here you could sense a determination, an undercurrent so strong that it would have scared me had I, too, not been part of it.

On our way in to town, we saw the women from the poor houses watching us with stony faces, and they joined us wordlessly. They felt the same urgency we did, the same hatred. They wanted donkeys to help them carry water back from the fountain, and not to have to spend all day carding, spinning and weaving burlap, linen and wool; and for fewer of their daughters to die the day they were born; they were fed up with having their masters chase them down and then put an end to the problem by giving them a bit of cash and abandoning the child; they wanted to marry—if possible someone who didn't smell too bad or hit them too often; they wanted their own homes, and as many children as God saw fit.

They all dreamed that one day, the heir of a house—any house, rich or poor—would fall in love with them and ask their fathers for their hand in marriage, not caring that they had no dowry or trousseau. That heir would be handsome, like Ramón, and strong but not rough, and he wouldn't drink or hit them or go with other women. In short, they loved Ramón and wanted him to marry Alba. They didn't care that she came from a rich house, or that her hands were fine and thin, or that she did her washing with Persil: they'd forgiven her these things over the course of the months they'd watched her cry silent tears while she washed clothes. These hard, stoic women, with square jaws and strong arms, felt in their hearts a tender, romantic air that not even they understood. Thus if Alba found happiness and married Ramón, it would be as if they, too, found happiness. Alba's tears had made her a symbol of all the women crushed by their cruel fate, and now they wanted to take part in the only romance to cross their paths. These are the *tionas*, women who will never marry because they have no dowry.

And so, immersed in a mystical communion of sorts, we advanced down the streets of our town, headed for Casa Torrera. And then, standing before it, we found ourselves face to face with the masters.

They, too, felt a wind sweeping through their souls, although theirs was diametrically opposed to ours. Where we felt hope, they saw danger; what we longed for, they feared; our happiness, for them, would have been misfortune.

For in our wretched land, the masters can feel superior only by dint of our hard luck: if they can't be rich and lead lives of leisure—as it's claimed some do in Andalucía—then at least they can compare themselves to us and take comfort. The men are masters and heirs, and the women are mistresses and heirs' wives; they are the ones who rule houses and decide how to administer poverty.

If a humble, rebel shepherd were to marry an heiress

against her own father's will, how could the old order pre-
vail? If such a subversion of logic and common sense were
permitted, where would it all end? What would they
demand next? If masters can't choose their own sons' and
daughters' spouses, what kind of authority can they have
over the rest of the house?

What's more—think the masters of the powerful
houses—Alba might still marry my son, and then our two
houses will be joined under my grandchildren. My blood-
line will be the most powerful in the land! That's the way
they think, and when a rancher starts counting the sheep,
crops and meadows he could gain, he gets obsessed and
can think of nothing else. No sense talking to him about
foolish young lovers who want to marry, or about love—
which he's never even experienced—or the dreams of the
downtrodden, the sorrows of the poor!

There they stood before us, the masters of the rich
houses, and their heirs. And there, too, stood the masters
and heirs of the poor houses, proud to feel they were part
of the landholding class and thereby set apart from those
who had nothing.

Impelled by the same force that had made me take up
cane and kitchen knife, they carried hunting rifles—many
of them the modern, double-barrel kind—and long,
Albacete knives hung down from their belts. And I'm not
sure how, but I knew their guns were loaded with the slugs
they used to hunt wild boar; and I could imagine what
would happen if they fired into the narrow street down
which we were advancing.

Crude mountain folk on the one side, crude mountain
folk on the other; it didn't matter if they owned land or
only dreamed of it, their faces bore all the determination

they used to survive the rocky hinterland in which they lived.

Neither faction was deterred by seeing on the other side their fathers, brothers, friends, schoolmates; we all felt the mark of Cain upon our foreheads. Shared blood would not stop us; on the contrary, one brother hated another for having condemned him to poverty or wrenched from him an inheritance that had almost been his; a son hated his father for having chosen a different heir, and a father his son for wanting to supplant him. The more the bad blood had been buried and suppressed, the more sign of it there was now.

I knew that the shotgun barrels would fire their slugs and the hardened shepherds would trample the dead and dying to set upon their masters. Then they'd begin a deadly embrace of knife thrusts and hatred, an embrace that ended when one or the other vanished from the face of the earth.

At that moment, I asked myself what it was that all that death could possibly achieve, what I was hoping to put right with my pathetic arms. I grasped the absurdity of the whole situation but was powerless to stop the impending slaughter. What could I possibly do, in the face of that ominous silence? Had it been a rational hatred, coming from people who think things through and discuss them, I might have tried speaking calmly and sensibly to them; but this was a visceral hatred, wordless, all the more fearsome as it flowed from the depths of their souls. So I slipped behind a corner to let whatever was to unfold, unfold.

Almost imperceptibly, Ramón signaled those following him to stop and he advanced with his mule towards Don Mariano, who stood fiercely clutching his English rifle.

They stood face to face, each staring into the other's eyes with icy rage. Then Ramón snatched his shepherd's crook from the mule's saddle, snapped it neatly over his leg and threw it to the ground.

"Not a shepherd anymore!" he cried.

By this he meant many things. He meant that he'd realized he could never save up enough money to marry Alba by tending sheep; that the ranchers had defeated him in that endeavor, but that he still wasn't giving up; that he no longer saw Don Mariano and the others as masters but as enemies to fight on equal footing; that he was renouncing society to set out in search of his own destiny.

After a silent stare-down that lasted a few interminable seconds, he turned, with his lame mule, and began heading north, to France. But before he disappeared from sight, he turned and shouted:

"I'll be back in two years!"

Nor on this occasion was that all he was saying. He was also challenging everyone, asserting that within two years he'd have saved enough money to compete with the Quixarel windmill, and the Larella place, and Ausuils' huts, and anything else that anyone in town might offer in exchange for Alba's hand. What's more, he was threatening unconditionally to kill anyone who married her before that time, and to kill Don Mariano if he consented to it.

Six words, in the mountains, is all it takes to express all of that. And I fear for anyone who doesn't understand hill talk, because those six words carry more weight than the solemn oaths sworn by people in other parts. Here, silence says far more than speech.

Once Ramón was out of sight, it was as if everyone were waking from a dream. The farmhands and shepherds were surprised to find sickles and knives in their hands, and wondered how they could possibly have ended up in town at that time of day when they ought to be out tending the land and cattle. The women looked around for their jugs and baskets, as if they had to justify to themselves having abandoned their spinning wheels and looms. The landowners stared in shock at their rifles, their faces flushing with a shame of sorts.

Of course, it was only natural for the townsfolk to be curious about what Don Mariano and Ramón were talking about; and nothing made more sense than to bring with them whatever tool they were working with at the time so it didn't get lost, and so no sticky-fingered neighbor prone to making off with other folk's things could nab it. And if a mob of hunters had at that moment gathered to set off after a wild boar, despite the late hour, it's only normal that they, too, went to have a look. After all, here in the country, nosiness is a venial sin common to all.

It was ludicrous! There have been masters and mistresses, *tiones* and *tionas*, heirs and—on occasion—heiresses, rich houses and poor houses, shepherds and ranchers, for a thousand years. That's the way it's always been, and that's the way it will always be, and everyone accepts their fate with Christian resignation. The town is at peace, almost nothing ever happens here, and all of that revolution business—that's all for foreigners, Russians who freeze to death and whatnot. Us, we're all family here! Still, Alba is looking a bit thin. Probably best to wait a couple of years before anyone marries her, anyway, and meanwhile her father can keep her well-fed so she fills out a little. Won't do any harm to wait awhile before any of us takes possession of Casa Torrera.

The poor folk, the same ones who moments earlier were prepared to face the landowners' bullets and slugs, to storm Casa Torrera in order to deposit Alba at Ramón's feet, now look bewildered, afraid of what they'd almost just done. Because like the landowners, they, too, want to forget; besides, they now see Ramón's challenge as an impossible feat. In two years, Alba will belong to Joaquín, the Casa Sosas heir, or any other heir; and the hope that they'd nursed in their hearts dissolved, leaving behind only resignation in the face of the stifling present, which seemed all the bitterer for how hopeful their dreams had been.

Everyone returned to work, downcast, and the street was left empty. And I sat down right there to mull it all over, and the knife concealed in my clothes weighed on my soul, for I couldn't fool myself the way the others did. But more than regret over what had almost happened, more than anguish over what would have happened if anyone had made an inopportune move, what concerned me was Ramón.

He was—in large part thanks to me—a young man who knew something of the world and, therefore, realized that France is not the promised land of milk and honey, but the other side of the Pyrenees, slightly—but not much—less poor than this one. And I'd been the one to tell him that for a young man whose only line of work is that of shepherd, the world is just as cruel wherever you go.

Then, too, knowing how contemplative Ramón was, I was sure he had hatched some plan, something only he knew. Otherwise, how could you explain the way he'd proudly summoned Don Mariano? And why else would he have bought a mule and shotgun? No, there was no way he was considering becoming a highwayman; that went against the essential honesty of his character. Besides, a thief doesn't live long in the mountains, not so much because of anything the Guardia Civil might do but because of the peasants' animosity. And even if he did, he wouldn't make much money stealing, because around here people's possessions are their houses, their animals, their land. So why had he gone north?

I gave up on trying to find an explanation and went back to work, since the kids were no doubt making merry in my absence, ignorant of the tragedy that had almost befallen our town. Then one of the windows of Casa Torrera caught my eye. I gazed at it closely and realized that Alba was there, behind the glass. No doubt she had seen what happened from her captivity; but unlike the others, who'd gone back to their everyday routines, she was still staring north.

CHAPTER VII

Ramón was going to become a smuggler.

Since before the time of the Celts, there have been traders on both sides of the Pyrenees, people taking animals and all manner of products from one side to the other, undeterred by the high mountains. When borders put an end to their early unity and the monarchs issued prohibitions and tried to hinder trade, mountain folks simply ignored any decree that flew in the face of their ancient customs.

In time, the monarchs gradually sent soldiers to force the people to respect their orders, and they in turn—also in time—began marking out secret routes that enabled them to outwit those attempting to sabotage their rights. Since that time, border guards and smugglers have played cat-and-mouse all through the mountains, the former fighting not only the harsh elements but also the animosity of the locals, who have never understood—and still don't—why they should have to pay anyone, even the King of Spain or President of the Republic, for the privilege of bringing a mule or a cowbell from Pau across the border.

Don't get me wrong, I'm not saying this in an attempt to justify smuggling; I'm simply trying to point out that neither Ramón nor his neighbors find smuggling in any way reproachable as a profession. To them, a smuggler is simply an honest trader who can get them some products cheaper on the other side of the mountain. They have no knowledge of, nor interest in, the treasury: look how much tax they pay on their land as it is! And what do they get for it?

A smuggler's job is dangerous and only the most daring or desperate dare take it on. But they earn money, good money, and Ramón was well aware of that when he decided to risk his life.

He was fairly knowledgeable about his new job, because shepherds and smugglers tend to be on very friendly terms. On the one hand, shepherds alert them to where the *carabineros*–the Spanish border guards—and Guardia Civil are, and play dumb when the forces of law and order interrogate them; in exchange, smugglers always have a spare bottle of cognac or a cowbell on hand with which to thank them.

The first thing Ramón did was to buy a few decanters of *anís* from a Spanish merchant whose name, I'm sure you'll understand, I have omitted. For the first time in his life, he had to argue and haggle aggressively: he didn't have enough money to pay for them, since he'd spent almost everything on the shotgun and mule. In the end, he managed to close the deal: the *anís* in exchange for half the cognac he brought back from France. Needless to say, it was a terribly unfavorable deal that slashed his profits considerably, but when it comes right down to it, if you start a business with no capital you can't be too demanding.

Ramón's first border-crossing was grueling and dangerous. He knew where France was only from the merchant's directions, and the coalmen and shepherds he met along the way were vague with him, not trusting a stranger. Plus, he didn't know where the *carabineros* might be keeping watch, or which routes were safe and which were not.

So he let his intuition guide him and, although his over-burdened, lame mule nearly fell over steep cliffs a few times, he gradually made his way to the border. Several times he had to dodge the *carabineros*, but it was easier than he anticipated, because by day his hawk-like vision—trained to scan for lost sheep—gave him a great advantage, and by night his exceptional hearing warned him of the smallest sound in time to sidestep unwelcome encounters.

Finally, exhausted more by fear than by the actual physical effort, he reached the dividing line separating the two countries. Although the moon was shining on the Spanish side—it was nighttime, of course, for even with his lack of experience he knew that the final leg had to be done under cover of darkness—the clouds amassed on the French side were bunched together forming what looked like a sort of dimly lit sea.

Now came the most dangerous part. Not only did he have to dodge the gendarmes but also—in an unfamiliar, foreign land—find the town where the trader who had an "understanding" with his Spanish counterpart lived. And all of this, guiding himself solely by the vaguest of directions. For Ramón, who'd been roaming the mountains since he was a boy, this was hard, but not impossible, as it would have been for me or any other townsman.

On the way back, laden down with cognac, he had a chance encounter that would turn out to be decisive. He was walking down the trail in the dark, faster than he had before since he no longer feared getting lost, when he heard the unmistakable sound of a horseshoe on stone, coming from a copse ahead of him. Immediately he left his mule between some bushes and prepared to fight, but the sound of snorting calmed him at once. He could tell it was a mule, and the *carabineros* (and, he supposed, the gendarmes) only used horses. It was a mule, and Ramón could have told us if it was tired or not, if it was a pack mule or not, even if it was young or not. He was also able to identify the footsteps of someone wearing sandals rather than boots, and by that time he was sure they were smugglers just like him. So he tied up his mule and approached the copse, humming a well-known peasant song, since that was the best way to avoid getting shot by someone you suddenly startled.

As he'd imagined, he came upon two smugglers with five mules, packed with merchandise they were taking to Spain. He greeted them in Aragonese, which caused them to remove their hands from their rifles, though they left them hovering close, and after a brief conversation, he explained that he was a shepherd who'd been fired by his master and wanted to learn to trade on both sides, as he euphemistically called it. In order to dispel their mistrust, he offered them one of his bottles of cognac.

One of the smugglers was uneasy, he was the edgy kind, and wanted to rebuff Ramón; but the other, who everyone in Spain knew as Pierre the Frenchman and who'd been smuggling for over ten years, liked the tone of Ramón's voice, as well as his frankness; and even though he couldn't give him a good once-over, as he'd have liked (in the woods at night not even a smuggler can see worth a damn), he told him he could accompany them until dawn.

And so Ramón discovered some paths he'd never have found on his own, and learned to wrap his mule's hooves in cloth when passing through a place where it paid to be stealthy.

When day broke and they'd been in Spain for an hour,

Pierre, who was at the head, motioned for them to hide on one side of the path. Hardly had they managed when a troop of five *carabineros* appeared, having changed their route in an attempt to improve vigilance.

As the guards passed, not suspecting a thing, the smugglers readied their arms. Any movement by just one of the mules would have led to their detection; luckily they made not the slightest sound, for these animals were chosen not just for their strength but also their unexcitable temperaments. There was no need to fight.

Pierre noted appreciatively that Ramón had taken aim with his old rifle and the barrel hadn't trembled one bit; the other smuggler, however, was still shaking in fear. Now that he could see him, Pierre liked the Spaniard's look: hard but not swaggering, quiet, resolute. He'd been of a mind to change partners for some time, because he didn't trust the one he had, too jumpy, and now fate was presenting him with a golden opportunity.

And that was how Ramón embarked upon the smuggler's path, and Pierre taught him not only to speak French, so vital for negotiations, but also the endless tricks and watchwords he used. Ramón learned that if a light was burning in the third window at the Benasque inn, it meant there were gendarmes nearby; and that the guard at a certain border post wouldn't send his men out on patrol at night as long as there was money left at his window each month; and that a certain path was so well patrolled that it was unwise even to take it.

He began earning money, lots of money compared to his miserable shepherd's salary. But he remained as frugal as when he was saving up to buy three feeble sheep a year; and when Pierre got drunk and offered him a drink, or encouraged him to have his way with a barmaid, Ramón simply shook his head in silence and went out to count the months that had gone by and the money he'd saved. And he hid this money someplace between France and Spain unknown even to his partner.

That spring he proved to be an obedient, diligent student, content with whatever he earned, even though at that rate he would never save enough money; but no sooner was he convinced that he knew every possible spot to seek refuge or hide from the *carabineros*, every path to France, every one of the places he could buy or sell merchandise, than he began to strong-arm Pierre.

At first not even Pierre himself realized. On waking up at the inn where he'd intended to get a few days' rest after a profitable trip, he'd find the mules saddled and haltered, his silent associate staring at him as if he were late. Pierre would get flustered and abandon the plans he'd made; and he'd say goodbye—sometimes—to whichever girl had been keeping his bed warm and then come out, mumbling excuses for having taken so long.

Soon the Frenchman began to find himself worn out, terribly worn out. And when he pondered the cause of his exhaustion—was he just getting old?—he realized that they hadn't spent more than a single night in the same place over the past few months, and they'd been darting back and forth across the border like a loom shuttle. What's more, now that he thought about it, lately each trip was getting longer and longer. Ramón always had an excuse to go a little farther: if we can reach the old Peña estate we'll be safer; they serve better food at the Coscolla inn; in Vallabriga there's better grass for the mules . . . And, of course, they didn't rest during the day either: since

Ramón didn't smoke—who's ever heard of a smuggler that doesn't smoke?—whenever Pierre stopped to roll a cigarette, it seemed Ramón was impatient as he waited; and the poor Frenchman, confronting his partner's penetrating eyes, ended up throwing down his cigarette half-smoked. So it's not surprising that what they used to cover in three days, now they did in two.

When Pierre came to the conclusion that it was actually his partner and not his health or his age that was responsible for his exhaustion, he tried to impose a more relaxed pace. But then he discovered that he was no longer the boss, not even close, and that his disciple was prepared to smuggle alone if need be.

A lone smuggler! Impossible. They all travel, at the very least, in pairs; and not just for back up in case of a skirmish with the Spanish border patrol or the gendarmes but to feel safer and not so alone in the hostile mountains. But Pierre remembered how he'd first met Ramón: alone, inexperienced, with a lame mule and a nearly unserviceable shotgun; and he realized that Ramón was totally serious. He became furious:

"What the hell's gotten into you? Up and down, down and up, no stops, no breaks, as if you had the devil on your heels. And what for? So you can hoard your pesetas and francs in some hidey-hole where they'll all just rot the day the *carabineros* riddle your big head with bullets! You don't even enjoy it! You don't drink wine, don't go with women, don't eat anything except those damn fried crumbs or bread and goat's cheese, don't buy nice clothes to replace your old skins, don't do anything at all! What do you even want the money for, anyway?"

"For a woman."

Pierre was flabbergasted. A woman? He had a long and solid history with inn and tavern girls. So his view of women was tinged with healthy cynicism.

"A woman! A woman! Why do you want to buy a woman if you can rent one instead? Don't be a fool, don't get burdened down by a woman who's going to order you around in your own house, and fill it with noisy kids, and look daggers at you every time you get a little carried away with another lass, and make a cuckold of you the moment you turn your back. They're all the same!" and he spit on the ground to underscore his contempt. "Good for a romp in the sack and that's it. I bet the woman you're talking about is rolling around in the gutter with some other fellow right now . . ."

Pierre, in his excitement, was blending French, Gasgogne and Aragonese as he spoke, peppering his speech with interjections in all three languages; and though he might have said too much as it was, he'd have said a lot more had he not seen his friend's hand close around the *faca* that always hung down from his waist.

Now, though I might be just a humble schoolteacher, I've tried many times to understand the intensity and nature of what Ramón felt for Alba. I've never managed to, perhaps because I'm getting on now and am disillusioned. Pierre, as far as I know, never managed to either.

Here in the mountains, feelings have a force and purity inconceivable to those of us born in cities. Of course, in cities, too, we fall in love, make enemies, and have ambitions; but scarcely five minutes go by before we see something in a shop window, or have to think about work, or get distracted by the latest affairs of state. So our love and our hate are but a pale reflection of what they could be.

The men and women from these parts, on the other hand, have no distractions, no shop windows, no radio, no newspapers; their hearts can be completely overcome by what's inside them. Feelings in the city are like wheat growing in a fallow field: it has to compete with a whole host of weeds and so never yields more than a few pecks; in the hills, though, feelings are like fruit trees: fertilized, pruned, tended so that not even a tiny thistle can steal any of their sustenance. Nobody here just rubs you the wrong way: you hate them to death; you're not simply taken with a woman: you love her madly. You'd die for a friend, kill for an insult.

Ramón had spent six years toiling and fighting for the woman he loved; over the course of those six years, she had filled every one of his days and nights. Every time he denied himself something, back when he was almost still a child, in order to buy a feeble sheep at the end of the year, he was laying the foundations of his love. Every frost he endured, every morning he went hungry, every exhausting step he took on those steep trails served to stoke his burning desire.

And in Alba's case, although I don't know it as well, I imagine things were the same. Her sensitive nature would rebel at the idea of being auctioned off, and in Ramón's love she no doubt found a sanctuary for her innate romanticism—the whims of a girl who, not content simply to marry, wants to be able to choose her husband, too. But then, over time, practically a prisoner in that enormous house, her only distractions the loom and wheel, her love grew stronger as the monotonous days deprived her of any other thought or hope.

If Ramón had been an heir, too, and Alba's father—logically giving in, since she was an only child—had paid more heed to his daughter's wishes than to offers made by other houses, perhaps they'd have turned out to be a miserable couple. Everyone knows that marriages of convenience are happier than marriages of love: since neither spouse expects anything of the other, they don't become disillusioned, and after many years together actually grow to love each another and forgive each other's defects. In marriages contracted out of love, on the other hand, after a few winters together it's hard for each of them not to become disillusioned with the other and, coming to despise the illusion that first dazzled them, end up despising one another. Or at least that's what the old folks in town say.

But when love must withstand tests and the lovers in question can barely even speak to one another, each becomes a symbol for the other, and they lose their earthly nature and enter the realm of ideals. Alba was, for Ramón, the compendium of everything lacking in his life: tenderness, sensitivity, affection . . . and he for her, in turn, symbolized kindness, devotion, a soul indifferent to the materialism that ruled the lives of the townsfolk.

There are those who speculate as to whether Ramón's love might not have been tinged with self-interest, with the desire to possess his own house in time. I don't think the idea ever crossed his mind, although no doubt the urge existed—unknown—deep in his soul, as it does in that of all the dispossessed. What I do know is that his desire to marry Alba had become the cornerstone of his life, his raison d'être. He couldn't give up his objective without simultaneously destroying his will to live. He had so merged his identity with the dream he'd harbored for all those years that he was no longer Ramón the shepherd from Casa Badiello or Ramón the smuggler but Ramón who loves Alba, who defies the masters, fate and the world for her love.

I think that Ramón was also unconsciously experiencing the rage and rebellion against the landowners that the peasants have kept hidden in the bottom of their hearts for millennia. And let's not forget that, having challenged Don Mariano publicly, his honor and dignity were at stake, too.

So Ramón found himself awash in a strange mix of love, hate, ambition, pride, idealism, and innate animal obstinacy. Nevertheless, accustomed to suffering hardships from a tender age, he not only endured pain and loneliness easily but also found the paradise that Alba personified that much more desirable.

At least that's the explanation I came up with for his superhuman perseverance. Of course, I might be wrong no one ever really knows for sure what dwells in men's hearts.

That's why Ramón, generally so peaceful, was ready to knife Pierre when he spoke ill of his true love. He simply couldn't brook such words, because if he came to think even for a second that Alba was a woman more or less like the rest rather than the idealized image he had of her, then his life and suffering would all have been for naught. Because Alba, to him, was like a damsel to a knight errant, the Virgin Mary to a mystic, and a houri in Paradise to a Muslim: the impetus for feats and for sorrows, the symbol of all things good that dwell in the human soul, the promise of future happiness.

Yes, now that I think about it, Ramón was out of his mind. Or, perhaps I'm just too old.

Pierre saw the deranged, murderous glimmer in his

friend's eyes and fell silent. Grumblingly, he agreed to follow Ramón in his frenzied delivery of merchandise; after
all, they were earning a lot of money, and within a few
months the snow would make the mountains impassable
and then they could rest.

Soon, on both sides of the border, Ramón became known
as "the Desperado"; without Pierre ever even opening his
mouth, people took one look at him and told each other
that all this was for a woman. Well, maybe he did say a
word or two one night after he'd had too much wine, or
perhaps he let something slip one night when he was in
bed with a woman who wanted to know why his friend
never came to her.

Despite their skill, with all that dashing from one side of
the border to the other, the pair had several run-ins with
both *carabineros* and gendarmes. But after a number of
skirmishes in which several guards ended up wounded, just
hearing the Desperado's name was enough to instill fear.

"No, sir, officer, we're not afraid. But the Desperado is
not your average smuggler, you know? You remember
Miguel, from the Bielsa post? Well, he's in the hospital
now with a lung full of shrapnel, and he had five men with
him and the Desperado only had one. And if we find him,
he's not going to run off and leave his cargo behind like the
others, he's going to set after us. And in the woods at
night, our rifles are less effective than his shotgun full of
slugs and his sharpened *faca*. We're not complaining, no
sir; but we make very little money and he's not afraid to
die, and a lot of us have wives and children to support.
Please don't send us out tonight; they say the Desperado's
in the vicinity; let's stay in the barracks playing cards and
drinking wine."

When the Desperado's fame reached our town—and we're a few days' hike from the border—we all knew who it was and why he had headed north that day. And against all reason, some of us began to dream that Ramón would succeed, and when Don Mariano invited me to his table I no longer found Alba's face lined with the tracks of her tears but shining with a glimmer of hope.

CHAPTER VIII

A lba wouldn't have been so happy if she'd known the state of Ramón's finances. It's true, he was earning a lot of money, more than he'd ever have imagined just one year earlier; he had at least eight mules—with all their trappings—to his name, and thus he could run all sorts of merchandise: *anís*, machine parts, car parts, cigarettes, cowbells from Pau, medicine, saffron, money . . . once he even smuggled car tires. In short, anything and everything that was priced fractionally different on one side or the other and could be transported by mule was conveyed by smugglers.

In four or five years of endless work he'd have reached his goal, but oh!, he'd said two years, not four or five, and there was not even the remotest chance that Don Mariano would grant him a reprieve. He added and multiplied a thousand times, just as I'd taught him, but life was forcing him to subtract and divide.

When the snow reached the mountain passes, Pierre, like every other smuggler, prepared to spend the winter enjoying the money he'd so arduously earned; but to his surprise, Ramón said he wanted to carry on making trips.

Pierre was furious. He called his partner many things: demented, greedy, foolish—though he also took great care not to say a word about the woman who'd caused his dementia, greed and foolishness. After shouting and swearing, he tried to convince him otherwise. He spoke of avalanches that take down hundred-year-old forests, blizzards that come on with no warning, slippery ice patches . . . to no avail! Nothing seemed to deter Ramón. In the end, Pierre said he was leaving, that he was fed up and that he wanted to live to a ripe old age and roll around with lot of women; and that it was clear that if he kept on with a partner like him, he wasn't going to do either of those things. So he harnessed up his mules, cursing all the while, and he left.

After a few minutes he was back. He flung his beret to the ground, stomped on it, cursed even more and, finally, said that Ramón was going to need an associate in France to receive and assemble shipments coming in and going out of the country, and he'd be the one to do that as long as Ramón was responsible for the dangerous part of the job.

Pierre paid some women to sew Ramón mittens and socks made of raw wool, so they wouldn't let the water in; he used boxwood to carve goggles with only a narrow slit to see through, so he wouldn't go snow-blind; he ordered a blacksmith to make spikes for the soles of his sandals so he wouldn't slip on ice-covered patches; he bowed strips of wood to make racquets so he could walk without sinking into the deep snow, and he ordered a compass from a shop in Pau so he could find his way even in a blizzard.

He taught Ramón about the different types of snow that hikers encounter high in the mountains, so different from those just slightly lower down, how some of them slide without warning and take down everything around them. Ramón learned to avoid sheets of ice that look solid but break when stepped on, not to stop at clearings in the woods, and a thousand other rules whose nonobservance could be fatal. And given that all of this knowledge still might not be enough to keep him alive through to spring, Pierre also lent him his Virgen del Pilar and Virgen de Lourdes scapulars and a tiny sack containing a piece of gauze soaked in consecrated toad's blood, which Mainela, the witch of Ansó, claims is guaranteed to steer you clear of avalanches.

Winter set in. Ramón carried on his back the merchandise that Pierre delivered to him at the edge of deep snowdrifts, where mules could no longer tread, and, weighed down with two *arrobas* of the most costly goods he could find, he'd begin the trek up to the border marker. And might I add that in Aragón an *arroba* is thirty-five pounds, not like in Castile where it's only twenty-five!

Panting under the weight, slipping, often falling in the snow, he manages to reach the hut where the Spanish smugglers await him. And there he collapses before the fire to let his socks and clothes dry, eats voraciously, sleeps the night through and, the next morning, returns to France loaded down with another two *arrobas* of merchandise.

When smugglers on either side of the border see him approach, they whisper to one another, "It's the Desperado!" in that reverential tone reserved for saints and lunatics. They rinse out his eyes with chamomile water to counteract the snow's glare; they soak his hands and feet in warm water boiled with rosemary and bramble to treat the blisters caused by the cold; they rub his face and lips with horse fat to soothe the burn that the sun and wind cause even his hardened skin; they apply macerated St. John's wort and olive oil to soothe the places where his leather pack has lacerated his shoulders; in short, those gruff men

treat him with a tenderness that would previously have
been inconceivable.

When Ramón leaves, sometimes in the midst of a blizzard, they watch him disappear and make the sign of the
cross—in part because they sense that within his soul lies
something they will never know, and in part because they
cannot fathom how he finds his way in the fog and snow,
for they've never heard of the compass his friend gave him.

The merchants go berserk. Now that there's no need to
wait until spring for that one item they need right now,
they bid against one another, doubling, tripling what they
would have paid in summertime. The smugglers deliver
the precious cash to the Desperado, not daring to siphon
off even a tiny bit more than what's theirs, for they would
have felt as if they were stealing ex-votos from the her-
mitage or the chalices from church.

And so winter's days ticked by, one by one. But when
spring arrived and the roads were passable by mule once
more, Ramón counted his money and realized he was still
far short of what he needed, and he had only one year left.

His body, which had managed to withstand every hardship thanks to his iron will, broke down when he lost hope.
He was now a rich man, richer than he'd ever dreamed of
being, but not rich enough.

Perhaps someone more sophisticated would have
known how to make the most of Ramón's money, investing
profitably in real estate speculation or the stock market,
but he was a poor shepherd who thought money could be
earned only by working or stealing, and so that idea never
even entered his head.

He spent a month sick and feverish, laid up on a pile of
hay, looked after by Pierre and the girl he'd brought to

warm his bed. The Frenchman groused and complained, but not too much because he'd earned a big stack of money after that year's frantic work; plus, he was tired, too, and the girl was very obliging, if a bit costly. They applied mustard poultices to Ramón's chest and rubbed his stiff joints with nettles, effective remedies that were as unsophisticated as the people who employed them; they gave him marshmallow and ribwort infusions, too, and fed him semolina and onion soup.

Although Ramón's soul had no desire to carry on, with their ministrations, his hardened body slowly recovered, until finally his fever was gone. But he remained pensive, brooding; he'd sit on a tree trunk in the sun and let time while away, as if his prior sense of urgency had vanished.

Then one day, when the girl was washing dishes down at the creek, Ramón said to Pierre, "I'm going to start running arms."

Pierre, naturally, shouted, protested, made threats and stamped on his poor beret. Arms! That damned Spaniard was going to get them both killed! It's one thing to smuggle a few goods right under the *carabineros'* noses—after all they were half-blind as it was and could always be bought off or scared off by firing a few shots. But what Ramón was proposing was another matter entirely. Of course, the unions and parties on the left were willing to pay for the arms and munitions they so desperately needed for their revolution—or maybe it was to defend themselves from the counterrevolution—and not only that but to pay exorbitant prices that would triple the profits they could earn with any other cargo. But what about the risks?

First of all, they'd have every snitch on either side of the border on their tails, and those men can't be bought off with a little cognac or *anís*, for they'd be paid handsomely if they blew the whistle on an arms shipment. What's more, they couldn't count on the smugglers' network for help, no matter how much they paid: the risks were just too high for anyone to accept.

Just crossing the border—well-known terrain for the pair of them—won't be enough and since they'll have no collaboration they'll be the ones who have to deliver the arms to a place where trucks can make a safe pickup, someplace near a well-traveled road; and that means going down to the plain and passing through a lot of hostile territory. If they have a run-in or, more likely, if some snitch runs off at the mouth, they'll have the Guardia Civil to reckon with, and even though they earn as little as the *carabineros,* they don't just run off when a few shots are fired. What if they get caught? They'll never be content with confiscating their cargo and sticking them in prison for a few months, no sir, if they don't shoot them on the spot, they'll put them in jail for years and years.

Did he even know what he was saying? How many trips does he think he can make before he ends up sprawled out on the ground, his body riddled with bullets? Two? Three? Forget it! And when Pierre says no, he means no.

And so it was that, three days later, Pierre found himself in Saint Gaudens negotiating with some unionists over the price of a consignment of rifles and bullets, as he silently cursed women for pushing men into doing such idiotic things.

Meanwhile, Ramón set about devising the route they'd take to the plains; and he decided that Biescas de Obago was the ideal place to rest the mules, due to its strategic location between the border and the lowlands. Maybe he was also influenced by the fact that he knew the terrain and the people so well; and of course, he no doubt couldn't resist the temptation to be so close to Alba, even in passing. So he made a deal with the folks at Casa La Selva, a small, humble farmhouse less than an hour from town; and they agreed that in exchange for quite a generous sum, they'd feed the smugglers and their drove of mules.

All spring and summer long, Ramón and Pierre ran rifles, pistols, bullets . . . to-ing and fro-ing from the trucks in Saint Gaudens to those in Lérida. And they were still alive. Pierre credited their miraculous survival—in equal parts—to his Virgen de Lourdes and Virgen de Pilar scapulars, the rabbit's foot he kept in his pocket at all times (the toad's blood being effective only against snowslides), and the incredibly good luck that lunatics like Ramón seem to enjoy.

But one day, Guardia Civil officers began appearing in town. Not the two or three who sometimes stop by to prove that, though it might be a godforsaken mountain town, even Biescas de Obago falls under the rule of law. No, there were dozens, maybe even a hundred of them. Some came on horseback, others had dogs, one even had a machine gun on his back.

They read out an edict in the town square, to the town's understandable uneasiness, and in it they ordered us to lock ourselves up at home and not come out, not even to water the animals. They warned—or rather, threatened—us, saying that anyone found out on the streets (or, worse, in the woods or open country) risked being shot if they did not stop in their tracks when told to. They also told us they'd shoot anything that moved, be it dog, mule, or person, after sundown.

As the day wore on, the guards set about rounding up the shepherds, woodcutters, coalmen, and pretty much anyone whose line of work required him to be out on the mountain, unconcerned about whether the cattle were penned or could wander into the fields, or if the coal bunker was lit and weeks' of work was going to be lost.

They were clearing the whole area; we all assumed they'd come to catch Ramón. For months, we had known that he sometimes passed through not far from here, though we had no idea of the nature of his cargo, or when and where he might come through. Don't ask me how we knew: it was just one of those rumors that comes out of nowhere and takes on a force of its own, until everyone is convinced that it's true, though no one can offer any proof.

Now there would be no friendly shepherd to warn him of the trap being laid around him, no markers on the road to apprise him of the mortal danger headed his way. Leaving a few sentries to guard the besieged town, the rest of the guards went off to set an ambush.

When night fell, I looked out my window and got the urge to rush out and warn him. But where was I to go? And how could I elude the scouting party—me, an old man with an arthritic back? If I'd scaled the church belfry to sound the alarm, would Ramón know how to read my anxious message? How could I get past the locked doors? What if it wasn't even Ramón they're looking for?

I spent all night in debating ideas of that sort, like every other person in town, all of us unable to sleep—the poor, full of fear; the rich, of nervous expectation.

It must have been about midnight when, out towards La Selva, shots were fired. First we heard the Mausers' sharp cracks; a few seconds later a hunting rifle fired back in response; then came cries of pain and the neighing of mules that had been hit; a little later came the roar of machine gun hail. And from my window, I tried in vain to fathom the secrets of the night.

Silence once more. And I buried my head under my pillow and cried, like so many of us did, as I wondered who it was that had betrayed him.

CHAPTER IX

I lay there for a few hours; I can't say for sure how long since at times like that you lose all notion of time. I marveled at how the world could be as it is, so unfair, so heartless—Imagine! Thinking that way at my age! And I told myself that Ramón would have been a thousand times better off if he'd just accepted his lot in life. I cursed those whose hatred and covetousness make the world a living hell, and I cursed the world that forces us to hate and to covet. In short, I raved.

And in the throes of that turmoil, I heard someone knocking at my door. I asked who it was (you don't just open your door to anyone after dark, especially that night), but I didn't need to hear the reply in order to know that it was Ramón. In my state of shock I slid the bolt open to let him through before I could think whether that was really in my interest.

Why did he choose my door to turn up at? Perhaps it was because the school is on the outskirts of town so it was easier to get to? Or perhaps in his desperation he was thinking back on happy times in his childhood, or when we used to discuss the current events in the newspaper? Or just because he trusted me more than anyone else?

When he walked in limping, his hands covered in his own blood, my spirit went into turmoil. For a brief second

I thought of the reward that the Guardia Civil would give me for turning him in, and the money Don Mariano would add to that. Delicious dishes of chicken, lamb, even fish danced in my mind; and a stove, a metal stove that would warm my house with no smoke; and a shirt—woolen on the outside and cotton underneath, the kind that are soft and yet so warm.

But a strange fervor overcame me, one that dispelled all images of meals, stoves and shirts. He sat on my chair and I saw that he'd been hit in the thigh, that he'd bandaged it up with a strip of his sash. We took off the bandage and, with a sigh of relief, I saw that the bullet had made a clean entry and exit. I cleaned his wound with water boiled with thyme and oak bark to disinfect it and help stop the bleeding, and then I bandaged it up again.

I cut up some bread and soaked it in wine and sugar and fed it to him. And after he'd eaten, he told me that he had to go, because surely the Guardia Civil would search the whole town to find him: he wasn't any old smuggler, he was the Desperado, and he wasn't smuggling cognac but running arms, hundreds of them.

Sometimes in life, the inexplicable happens. I knew that, given his leg wound, Ramón would never be able to escape, since they had dogs. So I said no, I told him not to go, to hide in my house instead; and without giving him a chance to refuse my offer, I began looking for a place to hide him, which wasn't easy given that my little abode is no big old farmhouse but a small room with a wood-burning stove and fireplace built onto the schoolroom where I teach.

Under my bed . . . no, that was the first place they'd look. I know! I unstitched my woolen mattress, and Ramón slid inside, along with his pouch and shotgun.

Then I stitched it back up—leaving a small hole on the side facing the wall so he could breathe—spread the stuffing out to hide the shape of his body, and then contemplated the results. A thousand nights I've cursed how little wool there is in my mattress, the way it bunches up and leaves the slats digging into my flesh, though now it looked like a rich man's bed, full of stuffing, not just a few meager threads like the beds in poor houses or dry straw like those of the disinherited. I sighed.

Yes, I know I was aiding a fugitive. I also know that if I'd been caught, I would have landed in jail and, even worse, would never have been invited to eat at a landholder's table again. As if that's not enough, if the story I'm now writing to unburden myself were to fall into the wrong hands, I'd run the risk of finding myself with no room and board as an old man. But, you know what? None of that mattered at all to me, not then and not now, because suddenly I didn't feel like I was over fifty years old, I felt like I did when I was a young, idealistic school-teacher who wanted to change the world. That same thrill was coursing through my veins, and my lumbago no longer hurt, nor was I fed up with eating slop, or tormented by my pending old age. Yes, yes, I know, it's not the same thing; it was of no consequence to History, to humankind, whether or not Ramón was saved. He was just a poor shepherd from a godforsaken town in the Pyrenees who was in love with a landholder's daughter, and that made no difference to the class struggle or to human freedom. But to me it was important indeed, because I'd seen Alba cry so many times, and I didn't want her to cry anymore. Me, I'll never again feel the tender embrace of a woman, and at best—if I don't spend too much on other things—I can hope to visit one of the town's sorry prostitutes from time to time; and yet, still, I wanted them to be able to love each other, and to share their dreams, and to touch each other like I did when I was young, though I've almost forgotten (or tried to). Because to me, they were like a flower in the desert, a sign of promise that brings joy by its mere presence, a message of hope, telling me that the world is not just a place of houses, cattle, land, hunger and hatred.

At dawn, the guards paraded the mules bearing the confiscated cargo through town; one of them bore the body of Pierre, the Frenchman who'd never again stomp on his beret and curse, because neither the Virgen de Lourdes and Virgen del Pilar scapulars nor the rabbit's foot had been able to stop the Mausers' bullets. Two other mules also carried corpses, which I later learned were those of anarchists who had accompanied the shipment in order to help manage the animals and protect the consignment in case of an unlucky encounter.

The manhunt began. Every house in town, even the richest, was searched from top to bottom by the forces of law and order. They speared haystacks with their bayonets, hurled the woodpiles stacked for winter to the ground, combed the barns, checked the oil drums . . . When they got to the school, all they did was look under my bed and open up the trunk where I store my meager belongings, considering that such a small space had so few hiding places.

Their futile search of the town went on for one day and one night. Then an officer read out an edict in which we were banned from leaving our houses and Ramón Gallar—also known as the Desperado—declared an outlaw, accused of contraband, armed resistance against the authorities, arms trafficking and conspiracy against the

Republic. The same edict warned residents that anyone who hid or helped him in any way would be considered an accomplice and prosecuted as well.

They finally left, taking the arms and the dead with them. A surge of relief flowed through town, not because Ramón had managed to escape but because everyone was frantic with worry about the animals left unattended on the mountain. That's the way folks around here are. Though at night they prayed for their hero to be saved— or captured, depending—the following day as the hours wore on, all they could think about was how thirsty the sheep must be, confined in their pens, about the wood- piles going to waste as they burned in the coal bunker, about the newly planted almond trees that the goats would demolish, left without a shepherd . . .

The moment the police left, everyone rushed to undo the damage resulting from nearly three days of nature free from man's loving care. I think if they'd seen Ramón bleeding on the side of the road, his shotgun slung across his back, they wouldn't even have stopped, as obsessed as they were with the work they'd be forced to abandon.

I ran to my bed and ripped open the mattress seam to let Ramón out from between the two pieces, yanking off the tufts of wool that had stuck to his clothes.

The first thing I did was examine his wound, and once I was certain there was no sign of infection and that it was healing as it should, I recounted to him his companions' fate.

Here in the mountains, death and life alternate so quickly—we're so accustomed to losing children and friends, our own end is always so near—that we bid the dead farewell with almost no sorrow, accepting it with the same fatalism with which we accept the cruel arrival of winter each year. Or perhaps it's just that hardship makes us selfish, wretched; we're so hungry that we have no room for more sublime emotions.

Add to this situation—common to all poor towns—the blind egocentrism of lovers, which keeps them from seeing any joy or pain not their own, and it becomes easier to understand why Ramón didn't cry at the loss of his friend and partner, instead simply lowering his head with a sigh.

He seemed to believe that if one chooses a smuggler's life, he knows death lies just beyond the next bend in the road. Pierre could have retired long ago, could have bought himself an inn or a little shop in any French town, but he'd opted to squander his money by treating anyone he could find to a glass of wine and sleeping with loose women, to keep feeling the thrill of outwitting the *carabineros*. You see, risk is like a drug: first you reject it, but then it pulls you in, and finally it controls you. Pierre had enjoyed his life of freedom, and he'd died before he'd gotten old and been forced to just sit on a bench weaving baskets. He'd have been proud of the fact that to finish him off they'd needed almost a hundred Guardias Civiles with horses, dogs, even a machine gun.

Ramón gave his friend no other funeral prayer than the one he'd have received himself if the tables had been turned, and thus his friend Pierre the Frenchman disappeared from his life the same way he'd entered it: silently. Such is the fate of those—like Pierre, like me—who help bring lovers together: oblivion.

Ramón himself had nearly been killed, too. Had the bleating of the sheep—a strange bleating, bleating of hunger and thirst—not attracted his attention, had he not left the column to go see what was wrong, he, too, would

now be draped over a mule's hindquarters with his friend
Pierre, headed for an unknown graveyard. But this, too,
seemed to leave him unmoved.

Even so, when I told him that the Guardia Civil had
mentioned him by name, he sunk into intense desperation
and silence.

The hours ticked by. I went to school, taught my
classes, had lunch at Casa Torrera with Don Mariano, and
we commented on what had just happened in town. Alba
listened wordlessly, staring at us with an intensity that
made me tremble. I'd have liked to tell her that Ramón
was alive, that he was at my house, but I could find no
opportune moment, for neither her father nor her governess left her side. Besides, I told myself, perhaps it's best
for her not to know and for Ramón to disappear from her
life once and for all, for her to reconcile herself to her hap-
less fate. But her eyes showed no sign of resignation, none
at all. And I realized that chance—or was it simply the
time-honored role she was forced to play as a woman?—
had dictated that she be the one to wait, to remain quiet,
to calmly endure like a tree in a storm. But she, too, was
capable of the same feats, the same madness as Ramón.
No, it was best that she not know where the man she loved
lay wounded.

That afternoon I finished teaching class and then, so as
not to draw anyone's attention with a change in my routine, I went for a walk, as always, to the Bolturella fountain. When I returned, Ramón was still sitting on the
bench, in the same position where I'd left him that morning, pale and silent. I lit a fire, since autumn was drawing
near and there was a chill in the air, and I put some water
in the cauldron to boil and prepared a little soup.

Ramón refused to have any, though it had been quite some time since he'd eaten. But then, comforted by the descending darkness—I don't waste lamp oil if it's not strictly necessary—he began to speak.

First he revealed the cause of his desperation: he'd lost Alba. Now he no longer cared if he got the money or not, because he was an outlaw. The Guardia Civil knew that Ramón Gallar was the Desperado, and he'd never be able to marry her. All he'd needed was to make one more trip, one more shipment, and by the end of autumn he could have come back to town with all the money he'd stashed at the border. More money than anyone around here had ever seen, enough to buy a house and all its land and cattle, money that Don Mariano needs desperately because even though he's got so much land, the ever-decreasing price of wool and meat makes it hard for him to cover expenses and pay his taxes. Money that, to a landholder, is more valuable than the Quixarel windmill or any fields. Money, more importantly, that he'd never have been able to turn down because with his silence he'd accepted Ramón's challenge, and to mountain folk, giving your word in public is more sacred than any contract written on paper.

Now it was all for naught because he'd been betrayed. It must have been Casa La Selva; they were the only ones who knew which day and by what route the mule train was to come through with the shipment; if anyone in the union had denounced him, the Guardia Civil would have ambushed him where he'd arranged to meet the trucks.

But there was someone behind Casa La Selva. Ramón paid them more than the Guardia Civil would have, and besides, no one would have risked incurring the Desperado's revenge if there weren't something important at stake, more important even than money: the rich houses.

A rich house can exert pressure on a poor house in a thousand different ways: by cutting off their access to water, refusing to employ their children, seizing their pastureland, letting the tax collectors ruin them. That's why every poor house has a guardian house, a wealthy house that protects it from the wickedness of the others in exchange for free labor and a degree of respect and submission.

But if all of the powerful houses were of a mind to crush Ramón and gave the nod, the pressure they could exert on any poor house would be unbearable. Once the suspicion had been aroused that Ramón was traveling via Casa La Selva, they'd have been subjected to an intangible yet tremendously effective siege: a few flocks of sheep accidentally trampling their crops without the guardian house interceding; a few stolen kisses when the girls went down to the fountain, to teach the master that his daughters could be raped and the town police would do nothing; a blacksmith so busy he wouldn't be able to shoe their mules for at least a month . . .

Finally, the master of Casa La Selva hears a couple of hints dropped at the bar and realizes that his house is being persecuted, and he knows they won't stop until they've destroyed it. At first he resists. He's made a pact with Ramón and to him this is very important; but one day he can't take it anymore and in exchange for his betrayal is granted permission to survive.

Ramón clenched his jaw in rage and hatred. It wasn't the guards he hated, since smugglers and the Guardia Civil in the mountains have always engaged in a deadly game of cat-and-mouse. Smugglers play their part, and the Guardia Civil play theirs: they're like two sides of the same coin. There exists a strange sort of complicity and respect between them, even though they might kill each other, because they each have to suffer the exhaustion of tortuous routes, the sun's blazing heat in midsummer, and the treacherous darkness of the night. No, they don't hate each other; and they feel a kind of sadness devoid of rancor when they take each other's lives.

Nor did Ramón hate Casa La Selva. He knew, better than I, the type of pressure they would have been subjected to. Really, they deserved his compassion, because now no one in town would take their word, not even those who'd forced them to besmirch their own honor. No one would do business with them unless it was in cash, or lend them money when they didn't have enough to cover their taxes, or wait until year's end to be paid for work done. Everyone hates a traitor, even those who have profited from the betrayal.

No, Ramón hated only the rich masters. Had he not saved up enough money in the two-year period he himself had set, he'd have accepted his defeat and left town forever. He'd likely have shared barmaids and tavern girls with Pierre and they'd have gotten drunk together and raced through life with frantic greed, defying death with every trip they took, becoming a little bit brasher with each success, until one day a few bullets finished them off.

But he hadn't failed, and the masters, fearing what his triumph might mean, had laid a death trap for him. Everyone had conspired against Ramón: the rich houses because they'd set their sights on marriage to Alba, the poor houses because they wanted to set themselves apart from the landless, and Don Mariano because he wanted to avoid the humiliation of being beaten by a shepherd who'd once worked for him, even though Ramón had brought him great profit.

That was why he hated them. He had forgiven the hunger, cold, misery, backbreaking work, and wretched pay, because all of that struck him as normal. It was all he'd seen since the day he was born and he couldn't imagine another life, one devoid of poverty. But now the masters had violated an unspoken agreement and that, in Ramón's eyes, was an abhorrent, unpardonable crime. By doing so, they'd made a mockery of him, of his buying his sheep one by one, traversing the mountains in winter, risking his life running arms.

If I hadn't held him back, he'd have made his way from the school through town, leaving a trail of blood and bodies in his wake until he was shot down like a rabid dog. In a cold sweat, his wild eyes staring at me unseeingly, he sat back down in the chair beside me. And in order to fend off evil spirits, he told me the tale of his love. The love he'd lost forever.

That was how I learned that he and Alba, hours after that first lighthearted kiss I'd witnessed, had kissed again; how they'd exchanged glances and messages that only they knew how to interpret; I also learned of their declarations of love and the fantasies they shared. He even talked of the first time they'd lain together one afternoon, hidden among the tall ears of wheat, and of how he felt, and what he dreamed of . . . The fact that Ramón, normally so reserved, should speak to me of his clandestine love, gave me an idea of how desperate he was.

As his tears for that happy day rolled down his cheeks,

his story came to the ill-fated moment when—he still didn't know how—Don Mariano found them out. The snow, hunger, and cold that followed—he withstood it all by thinking of her; and when the loneliness became unbearable, he'd look down on the town from up in the sierra and find Alba's window, open in the day and illuminated at night, providing the solace of a lighthouse, telling him that she was there, she was waiting for him, she loved him.

Then he described his time as a smuggler, particularly that terrible winter when almost all he could remember was how deadly white it was, how intolerably cold it was, the crushing the weight he had to carry, and how he still felt the dire need to take another step, always one more step, and then another, and another . . .

And jolly Pierre, his faithful partner—dead. It was all lost, all a waste, all for nothing!

I noticed that his hand was stroking his shotgun and guessed what he was thinking then: since the masters had forgotten honor, neither was he obliged to pay allegiance to any law—human or divine. I felt a chill run down my spine, for in his eyes I saw the determination to kill if necessary, to fight anything standing in the way of his obsessive love, undeterred by compassion or morals. And I felt a fear, an irrational fear, sensing the blind, unstoppable force of nature coursing through his veins.

Without another word, he sunk into an ominous silence and, pulling a long Albacete knife from his sash, he began to sharpen it with a little whetting stone he took from his pouch.

An hour later I went to bed, without receiving a reply when I bid him goodnight, without any break in the hypnotic rhythm of his knife, sliding up and down the stone.

The enervating sound of steel scraping across sandstone went on all night. I dozed off, tossed and turned, woke back up . . . and on it went. And for three nights, while his leg finished healing, Ramón hatched his plan.

I awoke with a start. Silence! Leaping out of bed, I rushed to the hearth; Ramón wasn't there, nor were his shotgun or knife. On his chair I found a wad of bills—several thousand pesetas, more than I earn in several years.

In gruff mountain talk, that money—surely part of his compensation for the arms shipment—said more than one might think. It said that Ramón was forgoing the challenge he'd issued to Don Mariano and thus had no need for all those pesetas to rescue Alba. But Ramón was not renouncing, would never renounce, his love. Now he was going to fight and kill for it, if need be. The money also told me that he suspected that I'd been tempted—out of penury—to turn him in, and that that he understood and forgave me. The money said that he was my friend. And, above all, it said goodbye forever.

Without even stopping to consider that small treasure, I threw on some clothes and ran out into the night, rushing to Casa Torrera to beg Ramón not to kill Don Mariano, not to turn into a murderer—for shooting an armed *carabinero* is not the same as killing a man in his sleep out of hatred.

Halfway there, I heard shots fired. Panting, I arrived at Casa Torrera along with a few close neighbors, and there was Don Mariano, clutching his English rifle.

It seems Ramón had scaled the boundary wall and gone through the patio without setting off the dogs, who knew him well. Then he climbed up a vine to his true love's window, which had no bars since it was on the second floor. He opened the shutters by slipping his knife between the two panels, and then with the butt of his rifle he knocked unconscious the governess sleeping beside Alba. Then the two lovers scampered down the vine and jumped the fence. But just at that moment the governess came to, since Ramón hadn't hit her hard for fear of cracking her skull. She screamed, alerting the entire house. Don Mariano rushed out onto the balcony with his rifle in time to see the two lovers racing down the street. And he fired without intending to harm them, for fear of wounding his daughter.

Don Marian's blood was boiling. Not only because he loved his daughter—which, in his own way, he did—but also because they had robbed him of his chance at the Quixarel windmill or any other equally tempting possession, and especially because the shepherd had humiliated him before the entire town. He could imagine their laughter as they said to one another, "They sure put one over on the Capon! Can't expect half a man to keep his daughter under control, can you?"

The rest of us—rich and poor alike—were too dumbstruck at Ramón's audacity to react. The possibility of the two lovers eloping was something that no one had imagined, although to anyone alien to mountain ways it might seem like a natural, logical solution. It hadn't even occurred to Don Mariano, for though he kept his daughter under surveillance night and day and didn't let her out of the house when he thought Ramón was nearby, that was just to keep her from seeing him and keep them from lying together.

So deep is the sense of possession here that everything seems to revolve around it: honor, marriage, children, hatred. Property is sacred, because our land is so poor, because every inch of earth is a struggle to cultivate, because so many more people live here than nature can provide for. For the sake of property, people here marry, have children, feud, work tirelessly; in a word, they pin all their hopes, even their lives on it. And since property is so zealously desired, property laws are the strictest and most respected of all, to keep us from killing one another. Consequently, fights can break out over the smallest encroachment on the far edge of a field, when the plow intentionally takes a detour; and this bit of stolen land, though it does lead to violent disputes, is never cause enough for murder.

If Ramón had taken bloody revenge on Don Mariano, everyone would have understood, because Don Mariano had broken his promise, and furthermore, his betrayal made Ramon lose both his many mules and their cargo. But stealing property as valuable as Alba was something no one could understand or justify. Nor had I, precisely because I'd lived here so long, guessed what Ramón was planning; the possibility never occurred to me.

Even Ramón had elected to endure a winter of hunger, become a smuggler and traffic in arms rather than commit such a heinous crime; and though in the end he'd done it, it was only after plumbing the depths of absolute despera-tion and becoming profoundly convinced that anything was justified by Don Mariano's duplicity. But by doing such a deed he had destroyed his own legend. He was no longer the shepherd who defied his master in order to amass his own wealth, nor the lover on whom everyone pinned their hopes, nor the daring smuggler who laid down his own laws. Now he was a thief—a worthless, des-picable thief. A thief who had to be destroyed.

"But what about what Alba wanted? Isn't she a human

being, capable of making her own decisions?" That's what folks who live in the city will be wondering, people who listen to Clara Campoamor's speeches; they'll find it logical for a woman to marry whoever she wants, perhaps even get divorced. But no, no human beings live here, and not even men and women. Here there are only households, and they account for everything, treat it all the same regardless: buildings, land, people and cattle. The will of Casa Torrera resides in one person: Don Mariano; and he decides everything, just as he himself obeyed his parents like a humble serf and had to marry the woman of their choosing. No, there are no human beings here, and when someone tries to act like one, it puts the whole community's survival at risk.

As for Alba, the rich heiress from one of the best houses in town, no one could understand her. It was hard enough to get their heads around the fact that although she was courted by every heir in town, she chose a shepherd with no inheritance; it went against all logic and common sense. But the idea of choosing to run away from home and thereby forsaking her inheritance was so alien to everyone's dreams and aspirations that it must have been brought on by sorcery or insanity. In a world where property is everything, renouncing it is inconceivable.

We were paralyzed with shock. But Don Mariano was so consumed by rage and humiliation that it overwhelmed his greed and, cursing all the while, he cried:

"I'll give my daughter to whoever kills Ramón!"

That was all it took. It was like ramming a stick into a beehive: the whole town began to buzz and stir in excitement, their hatred for the outlaw boiling over. The masters of the rich houses imposed their own order—they weren't about to let any old lout wed Alba just for firing a lucky shot—and soon the heirs of the eight most powerful houses in town were atop their horses in their deep, Spanish saddles.

They carried their boar-hunting rifles and wore cartridge belts across their chests. At their waists, Toledan daggers. Strapped to their saddles were blankets and knapsacks packed with bread for themselves and oats for the horses, in case the chase was protracted.

And their faces—hard faces, stony, every bit as resolute as Ramón's could be, but far more brutal. Disturbing thoughts could be read in their looks, their gestures, their very beings. On the one hand hatred, pure hatred, crystallized in their desire for revenge, hatred for the one who dares to dispute their supremacy, hatred for the humble who have rebelled. On the other, a sneering pride, a sense of superiority: they were the heirs, the future masters of the land, those who could afford to ride horses to local fairs rather than go by foot or mule. You could even sense their thrill at being so close to murder, a vestige of hunting that clouds men's minds and makes them act brave, and cruel. And greed, an unbridled thirst for land, an overwhelming desire to win the marriage that would not only make them the largest landholders in town but also mean that their fathers could never disown them and turn them into *tiones* at will.

What scared me the most was the excitement of lust you could sense in their bodies. Year after year they had put off getting married so as not to lose out on the chance to wed Alba and now they were smoldering with unsatisfied desire. They wanted to possess a woman and possess her brutally, on their enemy's blood. I shuddered, for I knew that if they caught the lovers, the victor would never wait for Don Felipe the priest to give their marriage his blessing; he'd rape Alba on the spot. The idea of her delicate body so defiled made me nauseous. I could almost hear her cry and beg in vain as she was violated; I wanted to vomit, wanted not to be in the company of those men, since I could do nothing to stop them.

What chance did Ramón have? The heirs were good shots since they went hunting every Sunday—far better than Ramón, who in his skirmishes with the *carabineros* had always relied more on his courage and the fear he instilled in his adversaries. Though Ramón knew the terrain, having been a shepherd, they were hunters, aware of each and every hiding place no matter how small, each bush that might offer protection, each cave and each rock. And they also had sabers and hunting rifles, not shotguns that were almost useless when it came to nighttime combat.

As the heirs prepared to set out, the masters went over their strategy in the flickering candlelight. One complained that the town raised only hunting dogs and shepherds, both useless for tracking men, but the others hushed him, saying it was no use complaining. They began to calculate callously, as if planning a hunt. Ramón must know they're going to alert the Guardia Civil, who will surround the area the following day, so he won't be able to stop, he'll have to try to make it as far as to the border where he has friends. They must be frantic right now, running for France, and they hardly have even a one-hour headstart; that's nothing for horses at a gallop. They'll be so fraught they won't stop to hide, and the moon tonight is bright enough that they'll be able to see them. Set the riders on them immediately!

Amid the cries and cheers of everyone in town, rich and poor alike, the avenging horsemen set off to restore peace, order and safety to the land, to kill the man who was to blame for their being jumpy at night and hating one another. Once Ramón was dead and Alba married to the man that birth had destined her for, then everyone could go back to living in peace—the poor without the torment of believing that their fate could be altered; the rich without the fear that their possessions might be wrenched from them. Everyone wanted life to go back to the way it was before. And for that to happen, Ramón had to die.

I saw them set off in the pale light of the waning moon. I couldn't even cry, my spirit was so distraught—not just over the near-certain death of Ramón and the misery of Alba, but over the hatred that was plain on the faces of the landless who had so recently loved them both. Distraught and alone, I cowered in a dark corner so as not to be near anyone; against all hope, I prayed for the hunters not to find them.

But they caught sight of them two hours before dawn, as the lovers were trying to hide a beech grove. The riders reached the edge of the woods, dismounted—their horses would only have gotten in the way there—and waded into the darkness, creeping slowly as if tracking a dangerous, wounded boar.

CHAPTER X

N ow that I've reached the part of my tale where I'll try to recount—and shed light on—the terrible events of Errosas forest, I'm not surprised that everyone prefers an impossible but reassuring explanation over the terrible truth, which leads us into the darkest corners of the human soul. Because what really scares the townsfolk is not just what the heirs did but the possibility—the certainty, even—that if they'd been there, they too would have done the same. That's why they close their eyes, because they cannot believe that the young men they saw every day in the fields and on the street could turn out to be such cruel, heartless beasts.

All I can say is that when the horsemen set off, their hearts were full of hatred, greed, lust and bloodthirst, as I've already explained; and I think these wicked feelings, amplified by the relentless chase and the darkness of the night, are all it takes to explain their later behavior. Or maybe Hobbes was right: Man is a wolf to man.

I'll try to write what I believe happened and the reader can decide which version is true: the one everyone else wants to believe, or the one that I alone, in secret, defend.

When, at the edge of the beech grove, Ramón turned back and saw the riders silhouetted against the stars, he knew they'd never escape; desperation seized his spirit and he trembled, wanting to give up and submit to death. But he took Alba's hand and they plunged into the darkness, for though he had lost the urge to stay alive—knowing there was no hope—he also wanted to keep feeling her hand in his for a few more moments, just a few moments longer, and to keep feeling her body near his.

A forest by night is like one enormous, hazy shadow. The faint moonlight cannot get through the treetops; men and animals that venture there must rely on senses other than sight, which can make out only blurred silhouettes. Neither the hunted nor the hunters can rush through the dark woods, for they'd soon get snagged on a thorn or tumble down a bank. No, though your heart is beating in terror, though you know death is on your heels, you must move slowly, so you can lift your feet high enough to avoid the snaking roots, so you can step gingerly on the deceptive, crunching bed of dry leaves before putting down your weight. Caution exhausts you, wears you out; your eyes water, trying to see in the impenetrable darkness, your bowels quiver, begging you to run, to throw caution to the wind and run.

But the hunters know better than their prey which paths to take; their boots are more practical than Ramón's sandals and Alba's shoes; their legs are stronger than those of a woman; and, most of all, though on the inside they're burning up, on the outside they're cold as steel: they're not the ones losing heart, fretting about their true love's fate, saying a prayer.

Little by little, the stalkers are gaining ground. Ramón can already hear their footsteps and knows they can hear his, too. Perhaps if he abandoned Alba, his agile shepherd's legs could shake off the heirs the way a deer in the undergrowth loses the dogs on its trail; but he's fought too long and too hard to sell his love for his life now: he'd rather die. Maybe by having Alba at his side, he'd have a chance at thwarting the hunters, for it would be hard for them to shoot without hitting her, too. But no, he can't do that; he knows the terrible wounds caused by slugs too well to expose his beloved to the risk of being shot.

So he whispers into her ear, tells her where the money is hidden, which trusty smuggler will help her cross the border and—perhaps—adds a few, very few, words of love, because the hunters' steps are getting closer, he can hear them. She weeps and worries, tries to run faster and trips, tells him she doesn't want to leave him and she'd rather die by his side; he dries her tears and tells her not to be silly, no one's going to die. It's just that he'll be able to fight better if he doesn't have her there to worry about. They both know it's a lie, that no one, not even Ramón, can take on so many enemies, but Alba says alright, she'll go, but he must leave her his knife so she can defend herself in case she gets caught; he senses that it's not for defense she wants it, but to take her own life when she sees her captors draw near. He tells her that he can't, that he may need it to fight, although they both realize that once Ramón has fired both barrels of his shotgun, his knife will be no good against his enemies' weapons.

The stalkers have heard their whispering, and now they know that only one person's steps are crunching through the dead leaves and presume that Ramón lies in wait. They smile. They'll get the girl later.

They ease their pace, creeping slowly so as not to give themselves away, using the trees for cover. They know that the first shot will probably wound or even kill one of them,

but they're indifferent; they're so possessed by depravity
that they just don't care. With so much hatred, greed, lust
and bloodthirst in their hearts, there's no room left for fear.

Ramón, too, is unafraid. Fear strikes when you fight
death, when you struggle to stay alive; but when you've
accepted the end as inevitable and await it, lying behind a
fallen tree, serenity floods your soul. If only they'd had
more time to get away! One more hour, by his calcula-
tions, and they'd have reached a safe zone; but the governess had sounded the alarm and now death awaits them.
He only hopes that Don Felipe is right and that there is a
heaven—or a hell—where he'll see Alba again; because if
there's one thing he's sure of, it's that if he dies, she, too,
will find a way to join him.

Suddenly a nearby snap interrupts his thoughts, forcing
him to forget his introspection and focus on the mortal
present. He watches a shadow take shape a few meters
before him. He stares intently; yes, it's a man moving
slowly, so slowly that he makes almost no sound. Ramón
calmly takes aim and fires just one shot; he rolls quickly to
one side as other shots are fired in response and the slugs
blast the spot where he'd been lying just a moment ago. An
anguished cry followed by a death rattle told him he had
hit his target.

He snaps open his shotgun to remove the spent cartridge, for if he fired them both he'd be defenseless. Then a
shadow moves toward him. Too late he realizes that this
hunter has predicted his move and now he can't defend
himself. He tries desperately to ready his gun, without managing to reload, and moves left. But it's impossible to dodge
the deadly slugs and he feels fire sear through his right
shoulder, jerking him backward.

The man who has shot him gives a triumphant cry and shouts that he, Enrique, heir of Casa Mariñós, is now the most powerful man in town and that he'll celebrate his wedding that very night, treating Alba like the whore she's proven herself to be.

Ramón feels the warmth of his own blood, his rage mixing with the sweet lassitude attempting to overcome him, and slowly, silently, he moves his gun to his left hand. He's only got one shot, but before he dies he wants to kill the man aching to rape Alba; infinite rage surges through his heart as he pictures her beaten, groped, violated by this man. Come on, come closer, just a little closer and I'll take you with me to the grave.

Ramón feels a warm spurt of blood spatter across his face as Enrique of Casa Mariñós jolts up into the air and flaps his arms as though attempting to fly at the same time an explosion pierces the darkness. Then, like a ragdoll, he flops back down. Now the dry leaves will be his deathbed, instead of his nuptial bed.

Everyone freezes for a few seconds in shock. Then it slowly dawns on them: the shot came not from where Ramón lies, as perplexed as the rest, but from one of them, one of the heirs. It was one of the hunters who fired.

They realize, then, that Enrique of Casa Mariñós will not in fact inherit Casa Torrera. And that any murder committed in the dark woods will go unpunished, for it will be blamed on Ramón.

They are the beneficiaries of their households, but in addition to their land, livestock and buildings, they've also inherited something else: hatred. Generations of hatred of the other powerful houses, unresolved disputes over property lines, missing cattle, insults gone unpunished. The rich houses present a united front because they hate the poor houses even more; but now the heirs are alone and their hearts are filled with the urge to kill, veiled by a darkness that will conceal any crime.

And not just hatred, but greed—greed that compels them to murder for an inheritance they lust after. Brutal greed, burning, destructive—greed comprised of a combined longing for possessions and for power.

And a sexual desire so long held in check that it makes them buck and fight like stud horses for a mare in heat, except that instead of teeth and hooves they've got deadly rifles and daggers. It's a physical urge that mixes cruelty with the pleasure taken in doing harm, inflicting pain and suffering—a wicked, animal desire that sometimes drives men crazy and turns them into monsters.

And blood fever. The red cloud that both excites and incites them to kill more and more, and to relish it. People say that when sharks smell blood, they go into such a frenzy that they're capable of devouring one other—that's what the heirs do now.

For when one man kills another, he doesn't leave it at that, but stabs him a hundred times, mutilates him, drinks his blood as if that might assuage the hatred of generations.

Amid the portentous dark of the forest comes the sound of gunshots, the wounded moaning, daggers piercing bodies with a sickening muffled thud. Silent, deadly shadows appear and disappear, stalk and shoot, kill and die. One attacks another without knowing his name; it's enough to know that he's a contender in the contest for land and power.

In the end there is only one heir left alive: Antonio of Casa Sopena, perhaps the most fortunate, or the most merciless. He has vented his hatred, mutilating his dead companions to avenge every offense—this one he's gouged the eyes out of for a dirty look he once gave, that one he's castrated for the time he ended up with the barmaid . . . his hands are covered in blood up to his elbows. And now that death and greed have been appeased, his lecherous perversion demands to be satisfied, and, impatient, he sets off in pursuit of Alba. He cannot wait to take possession of his just desserts.

But as he passes Ramón's bloody body, still holding the shotgun in his left hand, the shepherd manages to raise it, aim at his stomach, and fire. The shot, at such close range, rips him in two, splattering viscera onto the trees as his face registers the shock—more than pain or fear—of dying, now that he's so wealthy.

Ramón sits up and reloads with his only fit arm. And then, in the unreliable pre-dawn light, he looks around and vomits. Vomits not so much at the sight of the blood and the display of carnage around him—as a shepherd he's killed too many sick sheep for that to have an impact—but at the hatred, the almost palpable hatred impregnating the air around him.

He crosses himself to ward off the tortured souls. He's still trembling in pain and revulsion. Finally, stumbling, he sets out after Alba's footsteps.

Back in town, we were all waiting. On hearing those first far-off shots ring out, off towards Errosas forest, the townsfolk erupted in glee and I bit my fist in anguish. Then came the confusion, when more shots echoed: why so many shots to kill a single man? When time passed and the heirs still hadn't returned, uneasiness began to set in. Day was breaking and yet no one resolved to go see what had happened; the landowners alternated between cursing and offering rewards; still, they themselves made no move, either.

Finally, they sent a messenger to inform the Guardia Civil that the Desperado was in the vicinity. Shortly before dusk, the guards arrived. Like the last time, they brought dogs, horses and their machine gun, but this time they realized there was no need to lock folks in their homes. When we told them what had happened, the officer ordered those on horseback to spread out and circle the area, forming a barricade so the fugitive couldn't reach France. Those with the dogs, on foot, were sent to the beech grove—and followed by every concerned inhabitant of the municipality.

At the edge of the woods we found the eight horses, their halters hobbled to low-lying tree branches in an orderly fashion. When we reached the place where the corpses lay, a shudder of fear and horror passed through us all. It was simply not possible that this whole cruel, sadistic slaughter was the work of one man: blood everywhere, bodies destroyed by knife wounds, amputated limbs, unrecognizable, disfigured faces . . .

A rumor began to circulate; perhaps one old woman first whispered it to another, and it swelled until it spread even to the Guardia Civil: the bear-man!

Legend has it that in the Pyrenees, just as elsewhere there are werewolves, some men turn into bears, and then weapons are no good against them. How else to explain that the town's eight best hunters had all been ripped to shreds? Their rifles had been fired and these weren't men who often missed when they shot, even at night. And their daggers, many of them unsheathed and blood-soaked, proved that they'd defended themselves in desperate hand-to-hand combat before being torn to pieces.

The commanding officer and I tried to point out that bear-men—if they even exist—have no reason to fire slugs into their victims before they set upon them, but no one listened. They were too scared. They clustered around Don Felipe, and men and women alike began to pray the rosary. Meanwhile the guards, uneasy, clutched their rifles as if at any moment a monster might come out and devour them.

Finally, the officer sighed and looked at the townsfolk. He saw that many of them intuited what had happened but preferred to cling to a legend. Then he glanced at me as if to say, better not to arouse more revenge and more murder; and he scanned the notes he'd taken one last time before ripping them up.

For all concerned—except the truth, and me—it was better for Ramón to be the lone assassin.

The officer ordered them to set the dogs on his trail as the townsfolk returned home, carrying the dead on improvised stretchers.

It seems the dogs led the Guardia Civil to some rocks, where they found the bloodstained strips of a woman's dress, as if someone had tried to make impromptu bandages. Later both trails disappeared into the Taona creek.

The Guardia Civil conducted a thorough manhunt. But what could they expect to achieve? National guards weren't afraid of any smuggler no matter how famous he might be; but against a ferocious, supernatural being that neither bullets nor daggers could kill, they felt defenseless. By night, the men crowded together around the fire rather than lie in ambush in the shadows; by day, they tramped along unwillingly, not stopping to examine bushes or bramble patches, clasping their scapulars tightly.

Three days later the officer called off the search, and when the guards passed through the streets of our town, I could see the relief at abandoning the manhunt on each of their faces. By contrast, a grave silence overcame the townspeople.

I imagine—although I can't know for certain—that after managing to elude the Guardia Civil, Ramón recovered from his wounds in one of the fields in the upper valley, fed and sheltered by his accomplices. He may even have used one of the newfangled medicines he sometimes smuggled, medicines better at preventing infection than rosemary or spider webs.

I don't often take notice of rumors, but they say that a month after these events, just before the snow cut off the mountain passes until springtime, all the smugglers in the Pyrenees—from Roncesvalles to Canigó—met up at the Balaitus pass. There, each one lit a torch and escorted the Desperado on his last trip across the border as a smuggler. All he carried with him were a few sacks of money, which he'd recovered in the days prior . . . and a woman. There was no way they were going to miss the chance to see the famous Desperado on his last voyage, or to get a look at the woman for whom he'd given up a magnificent estate, the one who'd inspired him to perform so many heroic feats.

Was it imprudent of them to light the torches? That was the last thing on their minds. These men didn't care if the gendarmes or *carabineros* caught sight of them, because the Desperado—the most daring, valiant smuggler in all of history—was with them, the man who's traveled those passes in the dead of winter, the one who not once but twice had dodged over a hundred Guardias Civiles who had horses, dogs and even a machine gun, the one who had killed the eight rivals who wanted to abduct his woman. What do they have to fear if the Desperado is with them?

As the gruff, hardened smugglers watch the couple pass, they feel something like jitters in their hearts and brows, as if they'd drunk too much wine; and they're surprised to find themselves wishing they could find a woman who looks at them the way Alba looks at the Desperado, so that they, too, could perform great feats, defy the world for her and lay treasures at her feet. Tomorrow they'll go back to being as brutal and materialistic as ever, but on this extraordinary night an air of romanticism envelops them, and more than one has to wipe the back of his weather-beaten hand across his eyes to catch a tear struggling to escape. These candles give off so much smoke!, they say to one other, not wanting to admit that they're moved by something so beautiful, something beyond their comprehension.

And so, amidst the smugglers' humble, silent homage, Ramón and Alba crossed the mountains and disappeared from our lives. Where might they be living now? Under what names? I don't know but, even if I did, I wouldn't say.

Are they happy now, a year after these events? I don't know that either. Perhaps, or perhaps not. Who can say? Not I, that's for certain. Men and women are still a mystery to me. But I wish them the best in the years they have left in this troubled world.

As for the other protagonists, the heirs have been replaced by their brothers, who are more than happy with this turn of events and have no intention of reopening a case that might trigger any bloody vengeance. As far as they're concerned, Ramón will always be the only guilty party.

Don Mariano, on the other hand, is disconsolate. Not only has he lost his chance at obtaining enormous wealth by marrying off his daughter, but now, too, Casa Torrera remains heirless. Don Mariano's brothers are all old now, and since theirs was a rich house, they went off to pursue their studies rather than stay here and end up disinherited *tiones*, so now one is a doctor and the other a lawyer—and neither they nor their children have any desire to be buried in this wretched mountain town.

Don Mariano is miserable, because he knows that when he dies, his siblings and their children will dismember the house and sell off every field and every cow to get the dirty money they appear to need so badly. He can no longer manage to work in peace; Casa Torrera loses more power by the day; now no one objects when someone's plow furrows a bit of his land or when others' livestock venture onto his meadows, and Don Mariano no longer even embarks on his amorous affairs, perhaps out of bitterness or perhaps because he fears some husband coveting his fields may decide to use that as an excuse to kill him and hasten their sale.

An undercurrent of alarm reigns in the town. The locals want to forget about Ramón—or to remember him in their own way, which amounts to the same thing. Because this whole story has awakened the ghosts lurking in our province and no one wants to confront them. It has shown us all a very dark side of our existence: the hatred of the rich for the poor, and of the poor for the rich; the hate of neighbor against neighbor; the hate of brother against brother. Hatred.

That's why they all choose to believe that Ramón killed all eight heirs, and that if he did run off with Alba, it was only because her father was the Capon, a half-man. Because Biescas de Obago is a sleepy town where almost nothing ever happens.

Readers will understand, now, why the townsfolk became so enraged at the *Herald*'s crude oversimplification. That poor journalist!, I think, to have to try to recount this story in a few short lines. You'll also understand the keen interest my fellow villagers had in putting forth their own skewed version and the despair that overcame them when they thought the world had snubbed them, when in reality, in these troubled times, nobody cares what happens—or doesn't—in a small town so far removed from civilization.

And what about me?, you'll wonder. How can I keep living in a place where such things happen?

Well, it's not such a bad life. It's true, of course, that people hate each other, sometimes with frightening intensity; but don't forget that Ramón and Alba were also children of these hills; people here love as fiercely as they hate, and when a love strikes up between them, it's so big that we city folk—we're more prudent, you see—have to turn away and blush, even if deep down we wish we could love with such devotion.

Besides, since I've been writing this story, I feel a warmth in my heart whenever I think of Ramón and Alba, and then I love my evening walk and the mountains and the trees, and the brats in my class and the old folks and the people who live in town, even if I know how mean they are; I even feel sorry for Don Mariano when he asks me over to lunch and can't say a single word without tears welling up in his eyes.

I'll never again know a woman's embrace; I'm too old now. But thanks to the memory of Ramón and Alba, without realizing it, without knowing why, I find myself loving the mountains that imprison us here and cause our hunger, the shady woods that strike fear in our souls, the cold creeks and even, yes, even the mountain folk who have had to withstand such terrible tests from such a young age and yet still find reasons to laugh and sing, and even dance once or twice a year. It's true that they're hard and vengeful and never forgive; but sometimes it's just the poor climate itself that makes them so wretched. Sure, the old laws they obey are cruel, stifling, merciless. But these people are also determined, loyal, frugal, long-suffering. And this blend of defects and qualities, superstition and wisdom, has kept them alive for over a millennium. And if at times they hate and kill, at least their hatred and killing is personal and concrete—over a piece of land, a woman, an offense—and they don't just kill someone for being of a different race, or from a different place, or speaking a different language, or having a different mindset, the way civilized folk do.

So why should I leave? Thanks to the money Ramón left me, I've now got an all-metal stove and a fleece shirt lined with cotton, soft and warm; and if one day no one asks me to lunch, I can afford to have chorizo and beans at home. No, I've got no cause to complain about my life, nor to leave this place. After all, this is a sleepy town where, as they say, almost nothing ever happens.

Lorenzo Mediano is a doctor, environmental writer, and the author of four novels. He was born in Saragossa, Spain, in 1959. His great passion is for the mountains he calls home, the Pyrenees.